SURVIVING THE WAVES
- A Convict's Journey

Historical Fiction
By
R.I.Maddams

First published in Great Britain in 2023

ISBN 979-8-8500-2570-0

Printed and bound by Amazon
Formatted by Softwood Self-Publishing

www.rimaddams.com

ACKNOWLEDGEMENTS

There are a few people who deserve a special mention for their help in making this book possible.

Curator, Olimpia Cullity, of the Fremantle Prison Museum.

Sarah Dronfield, at the History Quill, for her excellent Copy-editing work.

Nathan James, Softwood Self Publishing.

Carl Thompson, cover & web designer.

Michael Yarrow, for reading through my first draft, and offering his helpful advice.

Above all, Yvonne Maddams - Without her support, encouragement and belief in me, from day one, Surviving the Waves – A Convict's Journey, would never have made it to print.

CONTENTS

PREFACE

Having seen the 1864 newspaper report on the arrest and trial of Daniel Phillips, I spent many years wondering and imagining what became of him.

In 2018, I renewed my research into Daniel's life, and also into the life of convicts during that period, hoping to get an idea of the fate that was likely to have fallen upon Daniel. I discovered many things, including the surviving copy of a diary, written by the Surgeon onboard the convict ship that Daniel was transported on.

While this book is a work of Historical Fiction, many of the names, dates, and events, are true. For instance, the name of the convict ship, the early opening hours of the beerhouse, and the attempted escape. Also, the baby mentioned, did indeed go on to have a dramatic life.

Between 1788 and 1868, about 162,000 convicts were transported to penal colonies in Australia; almost 2,000 came from Hertfordshire. These convicts had received sentences of seven or more years, for crimes such as, murder, rape, theft of goods over a shilling, receiving stolen goods, desertion from the army, and setting fire to a barley stack.

During the mid 1800's, the Swan River Colony (later known as Fremantle), and the surrounding area's in Western Australia, lacked workers for the construction of much needed infrastructure, such as roads, bridges and other public works. It was for this reason that the convicts were transported there, as a cheap form of labour. From 1850 to the beginning of 1858, some 9,700 convicts were transported to Western Australia.

After their release, some convicts were fortunate enough to have family members settle with them in Australia. However very few of these convicts were ever able to return home to Britain.

CHAPTER 1

A Christmas Visit

Abigail, aged nine, and Archie, aged six, bounded into the kitchen, giggling with excitement. Father Christmas had left two presents on the breakfast table.

'Have something to eat, before you open the presents,' called out their mother, Lesley, as she was opening the oven door, releasing the smell of freshly baked croissants.

Stephen, the children's father, opened a new jar of home-made strawberry jam, ready to accompany the tasty delights that were now on their way from the oven.

The children quickly devoured their breakfast, and before the last morsel had been swallowed, they began opening their gifts. Abigail ripped open the Christmas paper, revealing a small, pink handbag. She now felt very grown up! Archie had been given a remote-controlled car, which he had been wishing for, and soon had it out of the box.

This had been the second round of present opening. The first round, the Christmas stockings, had already been completed, and their contents were now strewn over the bedroom floor.

'Right, come on, both of you,' said Lesley. 'Up those stairs and get dressed. We need to leave for Granny and Grandad's in less than an hour.'

Normally it was somewhat of a battle trying to get the children dressed in the morning, especially if it was a school morning! But going to their grandparents' on Christmas Day was the one day each year when Lesley knew there would be no such battle.

An hour later Stephen was outside, re-arranging a car boot full of gifts for the umpteenth time. So far he had failed with his attempts to shut the boot without fear of crushing something within. It wasn't just the gifts for his parents they were taking with them. There were also many more for the children.

This had now become a family tradition which not only gave the children more time to appreciate each gift as they were opened, it also helped spread out the Christmas fun and excitement throughout the day. They would usually open some before dinner, then gifts from their grandparents after dinner, and remaining ones shortly before they headed back home in the evening.

Just as Stephen was feeling that he might, with a little bit of luck, be able to safely close the boot of the car, Lesley and the children came out of the house. They were all dressed in their new Christmas finery. Archie was carrying his remote-controlled car, and Abigail was carrying her new handbag. Lesley had both arms around a very large box, wrapped in golden-coloured paper with a big tartan bow on top.

'This needs to go in too,' called out Lesley as she approached.

Stephen glanced around, turning up his nose as he saw the large present she was holding.

'Oh no, you must be joking. That'll never fit in.'

'It's Grandad's present. We can't leave it behind, can we?' she replied, before scrutinising the boot of the car. Realising that Stephen's judgement couldn't be disputed this time, she frowned.

'Oh well, never mind, I can have it on my lap, it will only be for an hour.'

'So I take it by that I'm driving, then,' replied Stephen with a resigned wry grin, and receiving in return a happy shoulder-shrug from Lesley.

With everything sorted, the family got into the car, and off they went.

After about three quarters of an hour, they left the main roads and began driving through a small village. If it hadn't been for all the cars parked both sides, along the entire length, it would have been a picture worthy of a jigsaw puzzle. There were several very old houses of varying colours, and a small village green, on which stood an old red phone box and a very large tree, which was adorned with large, colourful Christmas lights. At the end of the green, they drove past a lovely old church, which was on a sharp bend, then they continued up a steep hill and off into the open countryside.

This road, or rather lane, led towards the next village where the children's grandparents lived. It was a narrow, winding, up and down affair, lined with many trees, hedgerows, and high banks, which obscured much of the view. When gaps did appear, the view, which stretched way off into the distance, consisted mostly of fields, meadows, and small wooded areas dotted around. There were few dwellings to be seen, other than one or two farmhouses and barns.

About halfway between the two villages they came to a tiny cluster of houses which were scattered either side of a series of very sharp double bends. Although there were a couple of newer-style houses, the majority were either typical Victorian farmworkers' cottages, or ones that were considerably older – some two or three hundred years older. In the middle of this isolated hamlet was a small track. It ran closely between a small group of houses before following the edge of a field, ending up at a large farmhouse at the bottom.

As they drove through this little settlement, Stephen began to slow down by one of the Victorian cottages and said in a loud voice so the children could hear, 'You see that house there, the one with the little wooden gate? Well, that's where one of your ancestors lived many, many years ago. In the 1840s, I think.'

'Wow,' exclaimed Abigail, 'that's a long time ago.'

'What's an ancestors?' asked Archie.

'An ancestor,' replied Stephen, accentuating the 'or', 'is someone related to you, who lived a long time ago. In other words, the people who lived in that house were your great-great-great grandparents, or maybe even another great – something like that anyway.'

This new bit of family history information didn't really mean much to the children, but they still stared out of the car's rear window, looking towards the house.

Stephen continued driving, and as the house disappeared from view, he said, 'I think it was sometime during the 1850s, when the family who had lived there moved to Hadham. Into the same house where your grandparents now live.'

The children were quiet for a few seconds as they tried, in their own way, to understand all their father had been telling them. This was short-lived though, as their thoughts soon returned towards seeing their grandparents once again, and of course, to opening more of their presents.

CHAPTER 2

Family Heirlooms

A few minutes later they arrived outside their destination. After several failed attempts, Stephen eventually managed to park his car between two others without hitting them.

Their grandparents' home had once been a pair of Victorian farmworkers' cottages. Then about thirty years ago they bought the cottage next door and converted the two into one much larger house.

The children soon had their seat belts undone and were out of the car, jumping up and down in the garden with excitement, trying to hurry their parents up. While they were still bouncing, the front door of the cottage opened.

'Hello everyone, and happy Christmas,' called out Grandad George, beaming with delight.

'Happy Christmas, Grandad,' screamed the children excitedly, and ran over to him, flinging their arms around him in order to have a big joint huggle.

Their parents followed in a calmer fashion, with Lesley giving him a peck on the cheek and Stephen patting him on the shoulder. Both actions were accompanied by a 'Happy Christmas' greeting.

'We've got a car full of gifts as usual, but I think we'll leave them in the boot till later,' said Stephen as they all headed inside.

They found Granny Kate in the kitchen, busy cutting crosses in those important Christmas must-haves, the sprouts! She wiped her hands on her pinny before all the traditional greetings continued in turn, until everyone had been properly Christmas-greeted.

'So, who's for a drink then?' asked Grandad George.

'Coke, please,' answered the children in unison.

Grandad George raised his eyebrows towards Stephen. 'Something a little stronger for you, lad?'

Stephen twitched his nose up. 'I'd better stick with a coffee, I think – I'm driving. Although I might just have a driver's glass of wine with my dinner.'

'I think I'll have a tea for now. Better not start too early!' sniggered Lesley.

'Okay then,' said Grandad George. 'I will sort the drinks out, and you lot make yourselves comfortable in the other room. I will have these ready in two shakes of a lamb's tail.' Which the children thought was highly amusing.

The front room was looking very warm and festive, with a log fire burning, cards on the shelves, Christmas cushions on the chairs, and a real Christmas tree standing in the corner of the room.

The tree was fully decorated with a mixture of old

and new baubles, silver lametta, and multi-coloured tree lights, which were gently glowing and fading.

At the foot of the tree lay a vast collection of nicely wrapped gifts, waiting invitingly to be opened. The children immediately spotted them, and unable to contain themselves any longer, they darted across the room so eagerly they almost landed on top of them.

'Don't touch anything, you two,' ordered Stephen, rolling his eyes.

'We won't. We are only looking, Daddy,' answered Abigail with an innocent, almost angelic voice, causing Lesley to give a sarcastic, 'Mmmm, I'm sure you wouldn't!'

A few minutes later Grandad George came into the room carrying a tray with the tea and coffee on, followed closely behind by Granny Kate with two glasses of Coke for the children. The drinks were soon handed out, and they all began chatting about how the morning had gone for them so far.

Archie sat on the floor, drinking his Coke through an eco-friendly straw while gazing around the room at all the decorations. He noticed, under an empty armchair in the corner of the room, there was a small picnic-style wicker basket. Being nosey, he put his glass down and crawled over to it. He tried to lift the lid to see inside, even though he could see it was held together with two straps. Intrigued as to why it was there, he looked to see if anyone was watching, but they were all far too busy talking. He hesitated, then called out, so as to be heard over all the chatter, 'What's in this basket, Granny?'

The family stopped their conversation and looked over to Archie, wondering what he was talking about.

'Ah,' said Grandad George, 'I got that down from the loft last week, when I was getting the decorations down.'

With that, he went over to the chair, which Archie was now half under, and putting his hands either side of Archie's waist, gently pulled him out so he could get to the basket himself. He then carried it back to a long coffee table, in front of where the family were sitting, and using the edge of the basket, he carefully pushed out of the way two small wooden bowls that were full of crisps and nuts.

Satisfied there was enough space, Grandad George ceremonially placed the basket on the table, and with a little struggle undid the two leather straps. Before he opened the lid to reveal the treasures hidden within, he paused, adding to the anticipation. He then said, 'In here are lots of old family photographs, birth certificates, letters, and other bits and bobs. They mostly belonged to my father and grandfather, although some of the things in here belonged to my family who lived even before them.'

'Do you mean an ancestor?' asked Archie, showing off his newly acquired word.

'Yes, that's right,' replied Grandad George. 'I was going to show you these things after dinner, but as you've spotted them, I guess I might as well show you now.'

All eyes were focused on the basket, eager to see what interesting things were about to be unveiled. Grandad George slowly lifted the lid to reveal a jumbled mess of the items he'd just mentioned and more. On top was a small cardboard box, which he removed.

'Cor,' exclaimed Archie, as Grandad George removed three medals from the box. One of them looked like a bronze star with a red-white-and-blue ribbon. Another medal was gold in colour, with a multi-coloured ribbon, and the third was silver, without a ribbon.

'I don't ever remember seeing all this stuff, Dad,' commented Stephen.

'It's always been kept in the loft, son. It's been years since I've had it down, though. You were probably a small child last time it saw the light of day.'

'Are they your medals, Grandad?' asked Abigail.

'Oh no,' he replied. 'They were given to my grandfather, for being in the First World War. He went to war in 1915 with the Bedfordshire Regiment, then a year later he joined the Suffolk Regiment. He was in France, in the trenches ... I don't know too much about what happened to him out there. He never wanted to talk about it.'

'He must have been very brave to have got all those medals,' suggested Abigail.

Grandad George nodded his head. 'Yes, he was. Although these medals were given to all the men who went to war. There was another medal, called the

Military Medal, which was given to men for doing very, very brave things. I don't think my father got one of those, but yes, he was indeed brave … In fact, all the young men who went out there were very brave.'

The room fell silent, nobody knowing quite what to say. Abigail peered into the basket, and seeing something which caught her eye, slowly reached towards a folded piece of rather old-looking paper.

'Careful with that, darling,' said Grandad, as he reached out to take it from her.

'What's that?' asked Archie.

'Well, this is an incredibly old letter. There are some other letters like this, written by the same person. I think my brother has those. Anyway, this one was written a long time ago, in 1866.'

Abigail looked over her grandad's arm at the writing on the letter as he held it carefully with both hands. 'That's funny writing, Grandad. I can't read what it says.'

'Yes, it is rather. That's how they wrote in those days'.

Lesley leaned forward to have a closer look. 'So, do you know what it does say?' she asked.

Grandad George gave a little chuckle. 'Well, we have a bit of a dark secret in our family. In fact, I'm quite sure that Stephen doesn't even know about this.'

Stephen and Lesley glanced at each other with raised eyebrows, and everybody listened intently as he continued.

'I'm not sure of all the details, although I can remember a lot of the things that my parents told me in the past. I believe it all started in the 1860s, when the son of one of our ancestors was a bit of a naughty boy. As a result he was sent to prison ... far away in Australia. He wrote this letter to his mother just a few days before he was sent there.'

Grandad George lifted up the letter, nearer to his eyes, and he began to read.

***

Dearest Mother,

When you visited me, a few weeks before my trial, I tried to explain to you why I committed the act. I am not proud of my actions that day. However, I still have no regrets, other than having caused you such anguish. But I still truly believe that the end result will be the best for me.

Mother, I hope by now you have been able to forgive me. If not, I beg of you to please find it in your heart to do so.

I am writing to let you know that I am no longer in prison on land, but on a convict ship. It's called the Corona. *We have been sailing along the coastline collecting other prisoners, but we will soon be setting sail to the convict establishment at Fremantle, on the Swan River. If I am permitted, I will write to you again when we arrive. Of course, this journey will take many weeks.*

It would make me very happy if I was to receive a reply from you, letting me know the latest news and especially how you and everyone else has been getting on.

All my love to you, Mother,

Your ever loving son,

Daniel

***

A thoughtful silence fell upon the room, with everyone's eyes following the letter as Grandad George placed it respectfully on the table. Stephen and Lesley picked up their cups, took a sip, and placed the cups back onto their saucers in unison, but still no one spoke.

It was Abigail who broke the silence with a soft, almost apologetic tone.

'Grandad, did you say that Daniel went on a ship called the *Corona*? ... I thought that was the horrible disease which killed lots of people all over the world?'

Grandad George gave a little smile. 'Yes, well spotted, Abigail. It is indeed the same name. The word "corona" is actually a very old word. I think it's Latin, and it means a crown.'

'So what did he do wrong and what happened to him?' asked Archie.

'And did his mother ever reply to him?' added Abigail.

'Well,' replied Grandad George, 'I'm not sure if his mother ever replied to this, or any of the other letters he sent. No doubt she would have been very upset at what he'd done and found it hard to come to terms with the fact she'd probably never see him again. Still, the letters must have meant a lot to her as she kept them safe for all of her life. As for Daniel, we may never know exactly what happened to him. Many tales have been passed down through the family over the years, though. Whether all the stories are true or not, I don't know. One thing I do know is about the crime he committed. This event appeared in a local newspaper at the time. A copy of this old newspaper still survives – it's kept in the county archives. I have been there to read it myself.'

'Oh come on, Grandad, please tell us all that you know,' pleaded Abigail.

Grandad George went back to his chair, took a sip of tea to clear his throat, then with everyone's attention firmly fixed upon him, he began telling the saga.

'The story goes something like this ...'

CHAPTER 3

Daniel's Story Begins

Monday, 11 January 1864

It was four thirty in the morning. Although dawn had not yet broken, the moon briefly appeared between the clouds, reflecting its light onto the blanket of snow which had fallen over the past few days. This caused a subtle aura of light to penetrate through the window of Daniel's bedroom, enabling him to see vague shapes of all the furniture in the room, and his brother, who was sound asleep in another bed.

Daniel Phillips was twenty-four years old. His father had died when he was five, and three years later his mother, Sarah, married a man called George Parker. Daniel missed his father, but George had always been a good stepfather to him.

Living at home with Daniel was a younger brother called James, who shared his room, and a sister, who slept in the bedroom next to theirs. He also had a stepbrother, also called James, who slept on a mattress downstairs. He would roll his mattress up every morning before storing it under Daniel's bed during the daytime.

Daniel had been lying awake for some time, deep in thought, reflecting on the lovely time he and his family had recently enjoyed on Christmas Day. However, at the same time, he found himself contrasting all these happy thoughts with how tough life had been in the weeks leading up to Christmas, and how much worse life had become for him since.

After a while he sat up in bed, staring blankly towards the far wall, mulling over an idea he'd been considering since the start of winter. At first it had not really been a serious one, but the more he thought about it, the more viable it appeared to be.

It had been during the church service the previous day when he had finally decided to put the plan into action. At first he had thought about carrying it out that same afternoon, but with it being a Sunday, the Sabbath, it didn't seem very appropriate. So he decided to sleep on it for one more night – after all, he knew that waiting another day was unlikely to make any difference.

Daniel finished weighing up the pros and cons of his plan and nodded his head slowly in agreement with what he had decided to do. His final contemplations over, he slipped quietly out of bed and began getting dressed.

Due to the bitter weather, he put on an extra vest, a thick woollen scarf his mother had knitted him for Christmas, and his winter overcoat. All of which had been hanging over the back of a small chair beside his bed. Picking up his gloves and cap, he crept out of the room and made his way downstairs, which creaked with every step he took. The door to the main room was ajar and opened without a sound. Slowly, placing one foot in front of the other, he headed towards the kitchen. On the way he gave a little titter on hearing his stepbrother breathing so heavily it was bordering on being a snore.

Daniel closed the kitchen door behind him, lit an oil lamp which was on the kitchen table, then laid his gloves and cap on top of his boots by the back door.

He then took the remains of a loaf of bread from a shelf, stuffing it into his coat pocket before returning to the kitchen table. He patted his trouser pockets, trying to determine which one had his money in. Identifying the right one, he took out the coins, gave them a little shake in his open hand, and began counting. Satisfied with the amount, he placed them on the table for his mother to find later. However, as soon as he had let go, he realised he would be needing a few for himself, so he took back two of the pennies. He began removing a third, sliding it towards the edge of the table with his finger tip. Just as he was about to tip the coin over the edge, into the palm of his other hand, he hesitated. After giving it a second thought, he slid it back to join the rest of the pile.

Daniel then took a long, purposeful look around the kitchen, trying to fix the scene firmly in his memory. Once satisfied he'd taken it all in, he went over to the back door and sat on the floor, making the lacing up of his boots a little easier. He gave the loops an extra hard tug to tighten them, and after putting on his gloves and cap, he opened the back door. Instantaneously an icy chill hit his face, causing him to give a little shiver. He left the house, very slowly closing the door for fear of waking up his family inside.

The pathway, which led to the small picket gate at the front of the house, was extremely icy, causing him to slip several times. Despite this, he managed to navigate his way down the path without falling over. Daniel shut the gate, looking back towards the house in the silence of the dark, as a new flurry of snowflakes began falling from the sky.

A few moments later he heard the sound of a door opening and closing from a nearby cottage. He assumed it had come from Levi's house, who was probably heading off to the farm at the far end of the village. Daniel didn't turn around, but kept looking towards his own house, studying it while listening to the crunching sounds of footsteps in the snow getting louder and closer. The sound stopped and a voice came from behind him.

'Morning, Daniel.'

'Morning, Levi,' he replied, clearly recognising his voice without looking round.

Levi lightly slapped him on the back. 'What you doing up this early? I thought you had lost your job?'

Daniel turned his head to face him. 'Yeah, due to my unsteady conduct, I was told,' he laughed, 'although it probably didn't help that I was caught asleep in the hay barn the day before! Having said that, I reckon with this winter being so bad, I was probably going to be got rid of anyway.'

'So why on earth are you up this early, then?' asked Levi.

'I'm off to Harrington's beerhouse, hoping to see John the shepherd up there before he starts work.'

'What do you want to see him for? He won't be able to get you any work where he is. Not at this time of year anyway,' stated Levi.

'Yeah, I know that,' replied Daniel. 'I'm just going to … well, just going to have a beer with him.'

Daniel and Levi continued chatting as they slowly trudged the short distance down to the crossroads. Here they turned left onto the high street, walking in the middle of the road, along tracks in the snow which had been made by various horses and carts that had travelled through the village over the past few days.

Great Hadham was one of the longest villages in the country, and as they made their way up the high street they passed several shops. Most of them already had a light shining inside, so Daniel and Levi were able to see the shopkeepers moving around, preparing to serve the village with whatever goods they would have to offer that day.

At the bakery, the baker was carrying a tray towards an oven, and a few yards further on they could clearly see the butcher sawing up a large carcass of meat. When they reached the middle of the village, the blacksmith had just started getting the furnace going in an outbuilding at the side of his old oak-beamed cottage. An orange glow surrounded its open door and swirling grey smoke was puffing out from within. As they passed by, Daniel nudged Levi and with a grin said, 'Look, there goes the breath of the dragon.' He picked up a handful of snow, and making a ball, threw it over the gate towards the door. His aim went wildly awry, hitting a large horse chestnut tree which dominated the yard, causing a small avalanche of snow to come tumbling to the ground.

A few yards further on was the Bull Inn. Carters would sometimes stop here to partake of a little refreshment during their journey from far-off villages, before heading towards larger places like Newmarket or Cambridge. Many of them carted hay on this trip, and on their return would be loaded with various other items which they'd been asked to bring back by the owners of their local shops or farms. To the side of the inn was an area where they would leave their horses. On this particular morning, two carts were standing there, but without their horses. A clear sign they had been stabled around the back of the inn while the drivers had spent the night in the small lodging rooms upstairs.

A few hundred yards further on, Daniel and Levi reached Cox Lane. This was not really a lane; it was more of an unmade footpath which had been squeezed between two houses. At the top it separated into several tracks which wound their way around the edges of numerous fields and wooded areas, giving unofficial access to a couple of small farms and outlying barns. Daniel and Levi shook hands, saying goodbye to each other before going their separate ways. Levi headed up Cox Lane in order to gather some things from a shed, before going to a large barn where he would be working that day.

Daniel continued on his way up the high street, until he reached another junction which had a road leading off to his right and a small lane on his left. This lane passed a few small cottages before coming to an end at a cluster of barns. From here, a series of foot-trodden paths, mostly unofficial ones, led to other outlying barns or official footpaths. It was one of these unofficial paths which Daniel now took, as he headed towards the beerhouse, in the tiny hamlet called Bromley.

Although it had snowed considerably over the previous few days, local farmworkers had been busy clearing the snow towards the sides of the lane, making Daniel's trek up it a little less awkward.

At the top, he was relieved to discover that the edge of the track he intended to take was covered with little more than a dusting of snow. This was thanks to the direction the snow had been blowing in from, and the thick hedgerows which had made a useful shield.

Not far from the beerhouse stood a field called Notley Wells. On reaching this field, Daniel could see the silhouette of a large barley stack in the distance. He paused momentarily, drew in a deep breath and exhaled with a long huff. Then leaving the footpath, he began awkwardly making his way across the lumpy, snowy field, in a beeline towards the stack.

As soon as he got there, he kicked it hard, twice, as if in anger. Then, almost tenderly, he began brushing off a little of the snow that was stuck to its side, then gave it a few gentle pats, as if it was a horse. Large snowflakes were now beginning to fall, drifting into his eyes, blurring his vision. Daniel wiped them off, then lowering his head to help prevent the snow from hitting his face, he continued on his way towards the beerhouse.

CHAPTER 4

Doing the Deed

It had taken Daniel a little under an hour to arrive at the outskirts of the small hamlet of Bromley. It was here that he'd been born twenty-four years previously. A few years later, when his mother married George Parker, they moved from Bromley to the next village of Great Hadham. Later in life, Daniel's work took him back to Bromley, where he had managed to gain employment on a farm. Prior to that, he had worked at Chaldean Farm, whose land bordered Bromley.

Just as the snow ceased falling again, Daniel came to the edge of a field, where a steep bank dropped to the lane leading to Bromley. Turning sideways on, Daniel attempted to descend the slope in an upright position. He'd only taken two steps when he fell backwards onto his posterior and began sliding all the way to the bottom. Gingerly, he got to his feet, hoping all his limbs were going to be working as they should. Fortunately he was still in one piece.

The lane had not been cleared for a few days, but a solitary cart had evidently been up the lane at some point during the night, as it had flattened a small strip of snow in the middle.

Daniel tried keeping to the track by putting one foot directly in front of the other. This proved a little difficult, but he persevered, knowing he should still make it to the beerhouse within quarter of an hour.

About halfway, he came to the home where he was born. He slowed down, staring intently at the house as he passed. He began recalling some of the happy times he had enjoyed there, like playing in the garden, climbing the apple tree, and feeding the chickens.

Shortly after passing his old abode he finally reached Harrington's beerhouse. He stamped the snow from his boots, took off his cap and gloves, shook the snow from them, and went inside. Sitting on a bench by the fire were three men, who eyed Daniel as he entered the room. One of the men, who had worked at the same farm as Daniel, called across the room to him.

'Hey, Daniel, didn't think I would see you up here again. You coming back to work with us?'

'No way, I'm not going back there ever again. I've got better things planned for myself,' replied Daniel, giving a teasing wink.

John Harvey, the shepherd whom he had come to see, was sitting by the window with a beer in hand. He raised it towards Daniel. 'Morning, my friend.'

'Morning,' replied Daniel, going over to the small bar, where he bought a pint of beer and a box of matches before joining John. He put his cap and gloves on the window sill, sat down, and took a big swig of his beer before putting it down on the table with a clonk.

'I've … I've got something to tell you, John,' he said with a serious look.

John wasn't sure if Daniel had really got something important to tell him, or he was simply messing about before coming out with something light-hearted. This would not have been surprising, as Daniel had a reputation for his dry sense of humour. He would often see the funny side of life in all sorts of situations, and was well known for his cheerful facial expressions by all who knew him. He had a cheeky grin and an open smile that was seen by many a lady as a highly endearing feature. His cheeky grin usually appeared on the left side of his face, an ironic grin on the right. He also had a very open, happy smile, which was usually accompanied with both of his eyes narrowing slowly until they closed. He used his eyebrows to good effect too.

John put his beer down on the table. 'Well, come on then, Daniel, what is it you want to tell me?'

Daniel suddenly began feeling a little uneasy regarding the matter he had come to talk about. Try as he might, he couldn't bring himself to look John in the eye. So, before starting his explanation, he fixed his gaze towards his cap and gloves.

'I've had enough of life here, John. It's either freezing cold or wet, and to make things worse, I no longer have any work. Even when I was working, it would be from first thing in the morning until the light faded. And I would still not have enough money to give my mother at the end of the week. At least not what I really need to give her to provide for my keep. Every year of my working life has been the same, and I know things will never get any better for me living here … So I've finally had enough of it all.'

'You're not gonna kill yourself, are you?' interrupted John, looking exceedingly concerned at what he had just heard.

'Nah, don't be silly, I ain't gonna do that,' replied Daniel, reassuringly.

'Join the Navy then?' asked John.

'Well, my plan does involve a boat,' Daniel said with a cheeky grin.

John leaned back in his chair. 'So, are you gonna tell me or not?'

Daniel took another big swig of his beer, before looking John straight in the eyes, and said, 'I'm going over the waves … to Australia.' He paused, looking to see John's reaction. Other than an unusually long blink there was none. So Daniel continued.

'There is a barley stack up on Notley Wells field, belonging to Mr Knight. I've heard the stack has recently been sold at auction to someone else. I'm not sure who to, but it's bound to be insured. Anyway, I'm going to fire it.' He paused again, waiting for some sort of verbal reaction from John. None came; he just sat there with his mouth and eyes wide open, still saying nothing, so Daniel continued, 'I know the punishment for this sort of thing is seven years, where I'll be spending about a year in gaol with hard labour, then transported to Australia to finish my sentence. But after I've done my time, I'll be free. Free to make a better life for myself out there. And what's more, in the nice warm sunshine.'

John shook his head in disbelief. 'Are you drunk, man? ... Either that, or you can't be of sound mind. Even seriously considering it means you must be mad.'

'Nope, I'm not drunk. This is my first of the day, and I'm perfectly sane!' replied Daniel, raising his eyebrows.

Daniel picked up his pot of beer, taking another sip before continuing.

'I've been thinking about doing something like this for a long time now. At first I couldn't think of anything I could do without causing anyone too much bother or hurt. Then, on Christmas morning during the church service, I had the idea.' Daniel gave an ironic grin. 'I saw the straw in the manger, and, well, that gave me the idea ... Okay, I know it's sort of wrong what I'm going to do, but at least I'm not actually hurting anyone, and like I say, I'm sure the stack will be insured.'

John leaned forward. 'Daniel, the owner needs that stack for his livestock, it's important this time of year. That's why you get seven years for doing such a bad thing. Also, once you've been transported, it's unlikely you'll ever get the chance to come back here again. C'mon, Daniel, think about it. And what about your mother and family, they'll be devastated.'

'Yeah, yeah, I know, I've thought about all that

stuff. I know it's gonna be a tough few years for me. But on the other hand, I've heard it said that much of the hard labour, especially in Australia, involves working outside on public projects. It will be warm, sunny, and I'll get three meals each day. Now you must admit, that's much better than life here, ain't it?'

John put his elbows on the table, with his head in his hands. 'Who else knows about this mad idea of yours?'

'You're the only one I've told,' replied Daniel.

'Please, Daniel, don't do it. Forget this whole mad idea,' pleaded John. Then, looking back up at him, said, 'Look, I'm sure I'll be able to get you some work with me, up at Lodge Farm in the spring. That's not too long to wait, is it? You've worked with sheep before, so I reckon I could get my boss to take you on.'

Daniel didn't reply. Instead he had one last gulp of his beer, picked up his things from the sill, and got to his feet.

'Wish me luck, my old friend,' he said, holding out his hand.

Reluctantly, John shook his hand. 'You will need more than luck.'

Daniel smiled. 'After I've done my time, I might go and find myself some of that gold they have out there. Then I will be rich at last.' He laughed, making his way towards the door. As he was opening it, John called over to him.

'Daniel ... Please, my friend, think about it a little

longer. Some men are kept in prisons or hulks for years before they are sent away. That's if you survive long enough to make the journey. They can be right disease-ridden holes, you know.'

Daniel stood still, with the door partly opened, realising that during his previous deliberations he hadn't given any considerations to any disease hazard which imprisonment might bring. John could see that his comment had made him think, yet instead of saying something to sow more seeds of doubt into Daniel's mind, he said, 'I must admit though, you could be right. I've heard rumours that once you've done your time, things can sometimes turn out much better for some.'

The piercing cold coming from the opened door was now sending a chill through Daniel's body. This, along with John's last comment, helped dispel any doubts he was having about possible dangers. He gave John a wink, and with his cheeky grin mouthed, 'Goodbye,' as he left the beerhouse.

As he was closing the door, for what he thought would be the last time, he heard John shout out, 'Let me know if it works out well for you, I might come and join you one day.' This greatly amused Daniel as he headed off back down the lane.

By now it was starting to get lighter. It was not snowing, but as he raised his head skywards, he could tell it wouldn't be too long before it was going to start to fall again.

Daniel crossed the road, climbing up the bank at

the same spot where he had slid down earlier. He then made his way across the snowy fields towards the stack which he had kicked on his way to the beerhouse. On reaching the stack, he crouched down on his haunches and began pulling out big handfuls of straw from the bottom, making a large hole in it. Then, gathering all the loose straw, he mounded it together, forming a small pile on the snowy ground, and sat down upon it.

He sat there, staring at the hole, almost as if in a trance, but with all manner of things going through his mind. His main train of thought was how his mother and the rest of his family would react when they got to hear about the deed he was about to commit. Thinking about all of this, literally in the cold light of day, his determination to go ahead with the plan started to wane. But just as his doubts appeared to be winning, more snow began to fall, and with it, his thoughts returned to the present situation he was in. He did not have a job, nor was he ever likely to get a settled job, certainly not one that would give a good wage. Also, having recently lost his work, he no longer had any spare money, and he was only too aware of the bad impact this was starting to have on his family.

There was something else on his mind too. Something which had been bothering him on and off for several years. He had known many nice girls during his life. Some of them were local girls, others had come to the village to work in service at one of the many large houses there. He was fairly sure that some of these girls had, at one time or another, taken a liking to him. He knew they loved his smile and cheeky grin, as many had said so in the past. Even so, nothing ever seemed to develop between them, at least not anything more than a simple friendship. So over time he had become convinced, whether rightly or wrongly, that they thought he would never be in a position to provide sufficiently for a wife. At least not in such a way that would give them some form of assurance of having a financially settled life.

Over the past few days Daniel had mulled over a multitude of reasons, both for and against his plan, many times, so he was well aware of the serious implications to both himself and others if he went ahead with it. He was confident that he'd prepared himself enough to withstand what the next few years would throw at him, but he was under no illusion: he knew it was going to be a hard period in his life, possibly worse than he was enduring at that present time. He also understood that in order to reach the land of his dreams, he would face a long, dangerous journey on a prison ship. A passage that he might not survive, either due to disease or drowning.

But each time he considered all these things, he ended up coming to the same conclusion. If he was to actually win the prize of a better new life on the other side of the globe, or at least have a chance of winning it, then he would have to go ahead with his plan. There was no other way.

So here was Daniel, sitting on the ground with a key in his hand. It was a key that would lock him up, yet at the same time would start to unlock another door. A door which would hopefully lead to the better life he had been dreaming of.

Daniel took out from his coat pocket the box of Lucifer matches he'd bought earlier from the beerhouse. He looked down at the box in his hand, knowing that once he'd lit the stack there could be no turning back the clock, as it would be up in flames within a few seconds.

His fingers were now beginning to feel painfully numb with the cold. So after removing his gloves, he began vigorously rubbing his hands together and blowing into them, hoping this would get the circulation going again. He knew this was needed for when the time came for him to strike the matches. It seemed to work, as the pain from his numb fingers, along with the waves of doubt, faded again, leaving him with nothing but positive thoughts of happier times which he hoped lay ahead.

Large snowflakes began falling once again. Daniel became conscious of a sharp, icy wind, blowing down the side of the stack, penetrating his clothing, causing him to shiver all over. He got up, adjusting his scarf as he surveyed the surroundings, making sure that John hadn't followed him and that the coast was completely clear. Not a soul was in sight.

Daniel knelt back down beside the stack, lifting his head towards the falling snow. Then, in as loud a voice as he could muster, he bellowed out, 'Australia, here I come.'

He leaned towards the small cave he'd made in the stack, took out a match from the box and struck it.

The match started to flame for a brief moment, then went out. *Is this an omen?* he wondered. *Maybe I shouldn't do this after all.*

But a wave of determination welled up from somewhere deep inside. Strengthened by this, he took two matches from the box, held them together, and struck them at the same time. They both lit up, burning strongly. Daniel held his breath while holding the matches close to the dry straw, until he was confident it had caught alight.

He remained kneeling, watching intently, as the cave of straw gradually filled with fire and smoke. Suddenly, without any warning, the fire began rapidly spreading sideways and upwards. The heat, along with the smoke from the fire, soon caused Daniel to stand up and move a few steps backwards. As the fire grew bigger, it became hotter, forcing Daniel to step further and further back. It wasn't long before he found himself standing at the edge of the field, a good twenty yards from the stack. Even at this distance he could still feel the heat, but it felt pleasantly warming. He continued to look on, mesmerised by the dancing flames, and entranced by the small pieces of black chaff which were swirling upwards in the air between the large white snowflakes that were drifting to the ground.

CHAPTER 5

Stewing it Over

Back at the beerhouse, John had finished his beer. By now he should have been at his place of work, but he'd lost all track of time. He was still sitting at the table, staring out of the window, looking above the treetops for any sign of smoke. He was unsure if he would be able to spot any smoke through the dark, snow-filled sky, but he kept scanning the view anyway.

John picked up his mug of beer. In raising it to his mouth he spotted something out of the window that appeared to be a small plume of smoke coming from way off in the distance. He gasped, wondering if it was just his eyes and mind playing tricks on him. He rubbed his eyes with the palm and fingers of his hand before refocusing on the same spot, but was left in no doubt as to what he was seeing.

'The idiot's only gone and done it,' he exclaimed, far too loudly.

There were now about a dozen farmworkers in the beerhouse. They all turned their heads towards John, wondering what his loud utterance was about.

Out of the corner of his eye he could see they

were all looking in his direction. He hesitated from explaining anything to them, as he didn't want to be dragged into the situation that was about to unfold. But realising he had now given the game away, he decided it was best to tell them.

'You'd all better come and take a look over here. I think Phillips has set light to a stack on Notley.'

All the men dashed over to the window, each trying to get a clear view, hoping to confirm for themselves if there was any truth in what John had just said.

'That's old Knight's field, where I work,' shouted one of the men.

'Quick, we need to save it,' called another.

With that, the men rushed out of the beerhouse, leaving their beers behind, heading towards the direction of the smoke. Apart from John, that was. It was obvious to him, judging by the amount of smoke rising above the trees, and its distance away, there would be nothing left of the stack by the time the men reached it. He was also feeling increasingly uneasy due to Daniel having forewarned him of his intentions. He feared this could be seen, in the eyes of the law, that he'd had some sort of involvement in the affair. After all, at the very least, he hadn't done anything to try to prevent the crime taking place.

Once all the men had disappeared out of sight, John casually made his way out of the beerhouse, leaving in the opposite direction of the fire. This was a slightly longer route to the barns where some of the sheep were being kept during this bad spell of weather, but as he was already late starting his day's work, he knew a little more time wasn't really going to make any difference.

**

The stack had now been alight for around ten minutes, and Daniel still couldn't see anyone coming towards the scene. So, assuming that nobody had spotted the fire, he decided to head off. His intention was to go to the top of Cox Lane, then follow it down into the village where he would go to the constable's house and hand himself in.

A few hundred yards from the stack he came to a large oak tree. Being of such an old age, it was sticking out prominently from the other trees which lined the edge of the field. He went over to the base of its trunk and, with his boot, scraped away the snow from between two thick, protruding surface roots. Having cleared most of the snow away, he dropped the box of matches onto the clearing. He smiled, pleased with himself for coming up with the idea, which he hoped would put him at the scene, hoping this would corroborate any pending confession. Daniel then took the chunk of bread, which he'd stored in his pocket earlier that morning, and began nibbling at it as he continued along the headland.

On approaching a field near New Barns Lane, he once again met his neighbour, Levi.

'Hey, Daniel, what's with that fire over there?' he asked, pointing into the distance behind Daniel.

'That's my doing,' replied Daniel, in a matter-of-fact way.

Levi laughed, but at the same time noticed the look on Daniel's face. He was concerned with what he was seeing, worried there may actually have been some truth in what he'd just been told. Levi mumbled a few half-words, struggling to find the right words to say, so Daniel stepped in to help.

'Sorry I didn't say anything to you earlier, only I reckoned you'd probably have tried to stop me ... I've been planning on doing this for some time. I really can't cope with life here any more, so that is my ticket to Australia, and a new beginning.'

'What!' exclaimed Levi. 'Ticket to Australia ... Don't you mean your ticket to seven years on the treadmill? A new beginning will be years away for you, if ever.'

'Well, it's too late now. I've done it, and I will just have to take the consequences. But hopefully things will eventually work out for the best.' Daniel gave a cheeky grin as a thought sprang to his mind. 'After all, there is gold out there, you know – maybe some of it has my name engraved on it!'

As he finished saying this, they both noticed the figure of someone at the far end of a nearby field, who was walking in the direction of the smoke. The figure was some distance away, so they were unable to clearly see who it was, but one thing they could see was the distinctive shape of a tall stovepipe hat. They needed no bigger clue than this to know it was the figure of a police constable.

'Will you come with me, Levi? I'm going to hand myself in ... Or if you like, you can hand me over to him. Then you might get a reward.'

Levi shook his head. 'No, I'm not doing that to you. I don't want any reward for this.'

'Just think, you could buy yourself a nice new pair of boots with it,' replied Daniel, temptingly.

Ignoring this remark, Levi said, 'Look, come with me back to the barn where I'm working. Just for a bit, so I can try and persuade you to change your mind. You could still say it wasn't you.'

Daniel grinned. 'It's too late for that now, I've already told John I was gonna do it.'

Levi bit his bottom lip, now firmly convinced Daniel was telling the truth, and it was probably too late to do anything about it. Yet he still felt the need to play for a bit of time, hoping he could find a way to change the course of events which appeared to be looming fast. An idea popped into his head.

'Listen, Daniel. You'll be going to gaol for this, and you certainly won't be liking the food there. So how about coming back to the barn with me? I've got a nice bit of rabbit stew saved for my dinner. I could soon have it warmed up,' he suggested, hoping this would be enticing enough to work.

'Rabbit stew? Are you having me on?' questioned Daniel.

'My wife made it last night. Like I say, it was for my dinner, but I could happily eat it now. No questions as to how I got the rabbit though. I don't want to be joining you in a lock-up tonight.'

Daniel's eyes lit up. 'Wow, I've not had rabbit stew for a long time.'

'C'mon then, before it's too late. This'll be the last decent meal you'll be getting for some time.'

'Well, I guess waiting a little longer won't hurt. Alright then ... Cor, I can almost taste that rabbit now,' said Daniel, laughing.

It wasn't far to the barn, so they were soon there, sitting on upturned pails, drinking a mug of tea, and partaking in what they both suspected would be Daniel's last meal of freedom.

As he was enjoying the stew, Daniel began explaining all his thoughts and reasons behind the destructive act he had committed that morning. Levi listened intently, without making too many comments, or attempting to persuade Daniel against the idea of handing himself in. For by now he'd already come to the conclusion it really was far too late for that.

After Daniel had finished eating, and had enjoyed a second cup of sweet tea, he got up from the pail he was sitting on, looked down at Levi, and said, 'So, do you wanna take me to the constable and get yourself a nice little reward, or not? You'd be stupid not to.'

'Huh, that's a bit rich, you calling me stupid!' huffed Levi, as he began fastening his coat. 'No, Daniel, I really can't do that. But I'll come along with you to see the constable. I don't want to miss this! Although having said that, if it's okay by you, afterwards I'll tell Mr Knight it was me who persuaded you to hand yourself in. It might help to keep me in his good books. I might even get a little extra in my wages at the end of the week … Although, knowing him, I doubt it!'

Daniel smiled, nodding in acceptance of this request.

'Thanks for the stew, Levi, it was lovely. I really appreciate it.' Then with pleading eyes he said, 'Can I ask you to do one more thing for me?'

'Depends,' replied Levi, cautious as to what favour he was about to be asked.

'Will you go to my mother as soon as you can? Explain everything I've told you. I was going to leave a letter for her, only I didn't really know what to write … So I didn't, but I'm now wishing I had.'

Levi gave a reassuring smile. 'Yeah, okay, I'll do that.'

He didn't really want to be the one to do this, but at the same time his heart went out to Daniel's mother and the rest of his family. He felt it only right they heard the truth as soon as possible. Although Levi knew that John the shepherd had also been privy to some of Daniel's confessions, he understood that it made more sense for him to inform Daniel's mother as, being a neighbour, he'd known the family for some time.

Daniel took hold of Levi's upper arm, giving it a friendly squeeze. 'Come on then, let's go back to the stack, see if the constable is still around.'

Levi returned the friendly gesture on Daniel's shoulder, and they made their way out of the barn, crossing the fields towards the stack, or at least, where the stack had been.

CHAPTER 6

Confession

On entering the field which adjoined Notley Wells, they saw a police constable over on the far side, who was coming out of a small wooded area which divided the two fields. It was instantly obvious that he was about to head in their direction. Realising this, Daniel felt his heart beginning to beat much faster. At the same time, his mouth became drier and was accompanied by an unusual metallic taste. *Why am I feeling like this?* he wondered. *After all, being arrested is what I want.*

He began taking a few slow, deep breaths, hoping this would help in calming himself down. It seemed to work, as the unpleasant taste faded and he began to feel a wave of calmness washing over him.

As they continued walking in silence, Daniel couldn't understand the feeling he was now having inside. It felt like the situation he was now in lacked any sense of reality, as if he was dreaming. Even though he knew this was no dream, as the effects of the cold, wintery morning weather were assuring him of that.

'It's Constable Newland,' pointed out Levi when they were about fifty yards from him.

Daniel had already fathomed this out, but on hearing Levi stating this fact, it seemed to snap him out of his dream-like state, and by the time they were face to face with the constable, Daniel was feeling in complete control of his emotions once again. Full of confidence, he spoke first. 'Morning, Constable. I suppose you would like to know who did it?'

'Yes, I would,' replied Constable Newland, with an officious tone.

'Well, I am the man who did it and no other.'

Constable Newland was astonished at his statement. 'You didn't mean to say that you did it, did you?'

'I did it, and right ought to be found out,' replied Daniel, nodding his head in confirmation as he spoke.

'Then, why did you do it?' asked the constable with a questioning expression.

'It was not done out of spite. I don't even know who it belongs to,' stated Daniel, shrugging his shoulders. 'I'd been to Harrington's beerhouse early this morning, and I did it on the way back.'

Constable Newland could hardly believe what he was hearing. He had been the village constable for a little over a year, and during his rounds had met Daniel and his family on several occasions. He had often engaged in conversation with them, and Daniel seemed the most unlikely sort of person to have done such a thing. So much so, he still wasn't sure if Daniel was telling him the truth. Although, as Daniel had now repeated his claim, he knew it was his duty to take the matter further.

'Come on then, Daniel, I'm taking you to the beerhouse. I want to see if they can confirm what you have been telling me.'

Levi started shuffling his feet, looking very uneasy, wondering if there was anything he should say. He was now starting to feel quite anxious, scared he would be seen as an accomplice to the drama. The thought did cross his mind that perhaps he should have spoken first and handed Daniel over.

'I wasn't with him when he did it, I met him afterwards. Didn't I, Daniel?' he blurted out, looking towards Daniel for backup.

'It's true, Constable. I was alone,' replied Daniel, affirming Levi's comments.

Constable Newland studied Levi's face, looking for any signs as to whether he was telling the truth or not.

'Can I go back to my work now?' begged Levi.

Constable Newland concluded that he had no evidence whatsoever that suggested any involvement by Levi, so agreed to his request.

'Yes, you may go on your way ... Mind you, I may need to speak to you again at some point. This is a very serious crime.'

Levi shook Daniel's hand, silently mouthing, 'I will let your mother know.' Then, at a fast pace, he hurried off, just in case the constable had second thoughts about letting him go and called him back.

Constable Newland reached down to his side, taking hold of a pair of handcuffs. On seeing them, Daniel knew what was coming, so he stretched out his arms as a reassuring sign he was not about to resist.

Daniel and the constable said very little to each other on their way to the beerhouse, as both were in deep thought. Daniel, wondering what would be happening to him for the rest of the day. The constable, still finding it hard to believe the confession that Daniel had just made to him.

As they entered Notley Wells, Daniel surveyed the area where the large barley stack once stood, which had now been reduced to nothing more than a pile of smouldering ash. A wave of panic hit him, as the seriousness of what he had done earlier that morning struck home.

Just as they were about to leave the field, Daniel remembered dropping the box of matches by the old oak tree. The evidence to back up his claim.

'If we can go back that way, I will show you where I put the matches,' Daniel said, pointing towards the large oak tree with both his hands, as they were cuffed together.

Constable Newland gave a tut, and a sigh, as it was now becoming even more evident to him that Daniel had been telling the truth.

'Why did you do it, Daniel? Surely you know what this will mean for you now?'

'The sky looks like it's breaking up. Maybe it

could end up being a nice sunny day,' answered Daniel, changing the subject.

The constable didn't respond, and they both continued on their way in silence until they had reached the beerhouse.

On arrival they found it was empty, apart from the owner, Mr Harrington, who confirmed that Daniel had indeed been at his premises that morning. He also repeated John the shepherd's claim, that Daniel had said he was going to fire a barley stack.

After hearing this, Constable Newland led Daniel over to where a small table and two chairs were in the far corner of the room. He made Daniel sit nearest the corner, making it more difficult if he attempted an escape. But given all the things Daniel had already told him, he was fairly sure this was unlikely to happen. Still, he could take no chances.

The constable took out a notebook and pencil from his top pocket, then began writing down all the relevant details and events of the morning. Starting with Daniel's confession, he then added all the bits of information that he'd gleaned from people whom he'd already seen before coming across Daniel and Levi.

Content that he had written down all the important details from his investigations, he returned the notebook and pencil to his pocket and said, 'Right, young man, up you get. We're heading back to the village. I need to send a telegraph to Constable Ryder in Stortford, asking him to collect you. We'll go via Notley, and you can show me where you put those matches on the way.'

As the constable was helping him up from the chair, Daniel gave a cheeky grin, saying jokingly, 'Can I have one last beer before we go?'

Unamused, the constable grunted back, 'It will be many a year before you ever have anything like that again.'

This notion had crossed Daniel's mind earlier that morning, while he'd been drinking with John, but at the time it didn't bother him. Yet now, hearing those words coming from the constable's mouth, it was something he'd have preferred not to hear.

***

When they arrived at the constable's house, Daniel was led into the front room, where a freshly made log fire was burning with vigour.

'Warm yourself up, lad. Take those boots and socks off too,' suggested the constable, with a brief nod of his head towards the fire.

Daniel didn't hesitate, for by now he was starting to lose the feeling in his hands and feet. Trying to remove his boots and socks with his frozen fingers, and with the addition of having cuffs on, was a far from easy task to accomplish, but he eventually managed it. He placed the socks on top of the fire guard, and stood his boots inside the guard, hoping nothing would fall from the fire and catch them alight.

As Daniel was straightening himself up, he heard a drawer open from behind him, and the distinct clinking noise of a chain. He turned to see what was happening. Constable Newland was walking towards him, holding a set of leg cuffs.

'Sorry, but I will need to put these on you too,' he said, holding them with an outstretched arm. 'After I've got them on you, I'll ask Mrs Newland to make you a cup of tea.'

'Thank you ... For the offer of tea that is, not the leg irons!' Daniel replied with a fleeting grin.

Constable Newland fixed the leg cuffs onto Daniel's ankles, then popped his head out of the door, calling out to his wife to make them a pot of tea.

It wasn't long before Mrs Newland entered the room with two cups of tea on a small silver tray. Seeing Daniel standing by the fire, she smiled a friendly acknowledgement to him.

In doing this, she spotted the restraints on Daniel but pretended, unconvincingly, not to have noticed, turning her head away as she placed the tray on the table.

Daniel had never engaged in conversation with Mrs Newland before, other than exchanging a passing greeting if they saw each other in the street. Even so, she was fully aware of who Daniel was, having become slightly acquainted with his mother and stepfather at various village functions over the course of the past year, since Constable Newland and herself had moved to the village.

Daniel thanked her for the tea, and she gave an awkward smile in return. It was obvious to Daniel that she was more than a little embarrassed on seeing him there in chains, so he felt he ought to offer up some sort of explanation.

'I've set fire to a stack up on Notley Wells,' he stated rather bluntly.

'Oh,' she simply replied and, saying nothing more, made her way out of the room. As she reached the door, Constable Newland gently called out to her and went over, whispering something into her ear. She then left the room, and Constable Newland poured out the tea. He handed a cup of tea to Daniel, and taking the other one with him, sat down in a comfortable armchair by a very full bookcase next to the door. Without saying anything, he pointed towards a small wooden chair near the fire and motioned with his finger towards the fire. Daniel rightly interpreted this as a gesture for him to move closer to the fire, and to make himself a little more comfortable. Which he gladly did.

'So what will happen to me now?' enquired Daniel as he sat down.

'Mrs Newland is going off to the post office, to send a telegram to Inspector Ryder at Stortford. Hopefully he will collect you later today. He will then take you to a lock-up somewhere. Possibly to a cell at the workhouse in Stortford.'

Whilst he was telling him this, Daniel glanced out of the window. He could see that it had not only stopped snowing, but it was now a bright and sunny morning. It dawned on him that this could be the last glimpse of sunshine he would be seeing for some time to come. Nevertheless, with it being so bitterly cold, he had no desire to be outside in it.

Constable Newland continued telling Daniel of his likely fate. 'Sometime, later this week, you will be brought back here to the village, to Gayton and Mott's. There you will be charged with the incendiary of the stack. You can expect to be committed to trial at the assizes, which is being held in Hertford, sometime in March.' He paused to allow Daniel to take in this information, then said, 'I'm not sure, but I would think it's likely that you will be kept in Hertford Gaol while awaiting your trial.'

Daniel remained looking out of the window at the sunshine as Constable Newland was explaining all this to him. Although he was listening, it felt as if everything he was hearing involved someone else's fate, not his own.

By three o'clock in the afternoon Daniel's clothes had dried out, and he was feeling exceptionally cosy, having been sat by the fire for so long. He had also partaken of two more cups of tea, some bread, cheese, and a tasty slice of Mrs Newland's home-baked cake. All of which he felt sure was not the usual fare bestowed upon Mr Newland's criminal intakes.

Several times, Daniel couldn't help but see the funny side of the situation. Here he was, siting in the constable's home, having committed a crime for which he was about to be taken off to a cell, and lose the next seven years of his freedom. Yet, instead of having begun his punishment, he was now warmer and fuller than he'd been for a long time.

CHAPTER 7

Locked Up

Constable Newland was putting another log on the fire when a sudden noise from outside caused both of them to turn their heads towards the window. Looking out, they saw the top of a horse and cart pulling up outside. Almost as soon as it had stopped, a policeman climbed down from the driver's seat, and no sooner had he disappeared from view than a loud knock came from the front door.

'Put your shoes and socks on, lad,' ordered Constable Newland as he left the room to let the newly arrived policeman in. They spoke briefly in the hallway before entering the room together. It was long enough for Daniel to put on his socks and boots, but not sufficient to finish doing up the laces.

'Phillips, this is Inspector Ryder,' stated Constable Newland.

Daniel noticed that Constable Newland had now used his surname, not his first name, or called him 'lad', which he'd been doing since arriving at his house. The constable's tone, along with his demeanour, had changed. He was again that very much feared custodian of the law. Not the person who had been present in the room over the past few hours. The one with whom he'd been eating and engaging in convivial conversations.

Inspector Ryder removed Daniel's restraints, replacing them with the ones he had brought with him. He then led him out of the house and onto the back of a police cart. He gave Daniel a couple of thick woollen blankets. A little aid, to help protect him from suffering too much from the bitter-cold winter air. Daniel was grateful for this, but having sat by a lovely warm open fire for so long, he knew they would be scant comfort, but better than nothing.

Constable Newland stood on his front doorstep, watching Inspector Ryder turning the horse and cart around in the street. As the cart came alongside the constable, Daniel called over to him.

'Thank you for everything that you've done for me.'

He acknowledged Daniel's gratitude without speaking, or showing any expression other than a slow nod of his head.

As they pulled away, heading up the road towards Stortford, Daniel yelled back, 'If you see my mother, please tell her I love her, and ask that she will forgive me.'

Constable Newland was looking towards Daniel but failed to respond in any way. Daniel was unsure if Constable Newland had heard him or not, so opening his mouth to repeat the request, he took a deep breath, but the cold air made him cough. By the time he had taken a second breath, Constable Newland had turned away, disappearing into his house and out of sight.

It was now starting to get dark. As they drove along the road, the warmth which Daniel had gained over the past few hours was rapidly disappearing. The cold air, enhanced by the movement of the police cart, engulfed him. He wrapped his scarf around his face and folded his arms around his knees, trying to make himself into as small a ball as he could under the blankets. Unfortunately this seemed to have very little effect, and a wave of gloom came over him, as yet again he began to grasp a little more about the severity of the situation he had got himself into.

Daniel felt sure that his mother would have, by now, learned of his deed. At least he hoped she had. On the other hand, he was deeply worried as to how she may have received the news, from whom, and what her reaction had been upon hearing it. He knew only too well how readily gossip could spread throughout the village, so he couldn't stop himself imagining what strange stories had already been made up. Or even worse, what could have been relayed to his family.

He desperately hoped that Levi had managed to see his mother first and told her the tale before anyone else had. That way, she would have found out what really happened and, most importantly, why. Daniel also clung on to the hope that once his family had found out the truth of the matter, they would understand and forgive him – at least within a short period of time.

As the police cart trundled along, Daniel sat huddled in the back, cold, in chains, knowing it was all rather pointless to keep going over all these things, as he was in no position at all to change the past. Nevertheless, he still couldn't stop himself from entertaining these thoughts for a few more miles.

Eventually they arrived at the union workhouse. Daniel was left chained up on the cart while Inspector Ryder went inside. He hadn't been gone long before he returned with two other men, one of which had a glowing lantern in his hand. Daniel had the blankets removed from around him before being helped down from the cart and taken into the large, dark grey building before him.

He was led along several narrow passageways before going down a small flight of steps. At the bottom, everything was pitch-black. Indeed, even with the lantern's light, very little around him was visible. But despite this lack of light, he was just about able to see that in front of him was a line of four or five doors. Cell doors, all of which were partly opened.

On being led into the first cell he was able to see a wall, about six feet in front of him, which had a long wooden structure fixed to it. This was to be his bed, nothing like the one he had slept in at home.

Inspector Ryder and one of the other men left the cell together. They stood just outside the open door, while the other man, who was holding the lantern, stayed behind. He produced a box of matches and immediately struck one. Then, stretching out his arm at full length, he lit a large candle which was in a metal holder fixed to the wall. Once the candle was alight, he threw the match down on the stone cobbled floor. Daniel watched the match as it stayed alight for a few seconds, then died. In his mind's eye, all he could see was that first match he had struck earlier that morning.

If I had stopped then, I wouldn't be here now, he thought to himself, but in a matter-of-fact way, still without the slightest hint of remorse.

The man put his lantern on the ground and began removing Daniel's restraints. After they'd been removed, he left the cell, slamming the door behind him, causing an eerie echo.

'I'll bring you some food and water shortly,' said one of the men from the other side of the door. Then all Daniel could hear was their footsteps fading away into the distance.

Now the door had been closed and the man with the lantern had gone, the cell became even darker. It took several seconds for Daniel's eyes to adjust to his new surroundings, which were now being lit by the solitary candle. Once he had become accustomed to the dim light, he carefully made his way forward towards the wooden bed and sat down. The cell was bare, other than the bed he was now sitting on and a metal bucket with a wooden lid.

If only I could be sitting by the fire in Constable

Newland's front room right now, he thought, with a deep longing to feel that homely warmth once again. Although he was no longer being exposed to the wintery elements outside, he had become so cold on the journey that he doubted if he would ever warm up again.

It wasn't too long before the door to his cell opened. The two men who had previously escorted him to the cell came in. As promised, one of them was carrying some food. Soup, bread, and water. Much to Daniel's relief, the other man was carrying two large woollen blankets and a small pillow in his arms. Daniel smiled, thanking the man who was carrying the blankets. It wasn't that he was ungrateful for the food which the other man had brought, but having already enjoyed the lovely rabbit stew earlier in the day and the sustenance he had consumed at Constable Newland's, he was now fully satisfied of stomach. Indeed he hadn't eaten so well in weeks.

As a result of all the drama which he had gone through that day, all he wanted to do at this point was to get some sleep. Which he achieved without any effort. After having first partaken of the soup, but leaving the bread and water under his bed for later.

Daniel spent much of the following day sleeping. This was a deliberate decision, as he felt it was the only way to stop his mind from constantly stewing over his immediate future, and what this unknown passage might bring.

While Daniel was having his lunch that day, he

began thinking further ahead, wondering how life might turn out for him in the years to come. Especially when he was free, on the other side of the world.

To begin with, he was feeling in a positive mood, coming up with several fanciful but uplifting ideas. Yet it wasn't long before he once again found himself dwelling on things which were more likely to be closer to reality.

In the past he had heard several tales about life in prison, not all hearsay stories either. He'd been given first-hand accounts, from three different Hadham men, who had served short periods of time in gaol for various, but less serious crimes.

There was part of Daniel that wished he'd asked them a few more questions at the time, as it might have put him in better stead for what was to come. On the other hand, he realised it was probably best not knowing what he might be in for.

CHAPTER 8

Committed for Trial

The following day, Wednesday, started in the same way as the previous day, with a breakfast of oatmeal gruel, eight ounces of bread, and mug of tea. After this he had a wash and wet shave from a bowl of lukewarm water which was brought to his cell. This wasn't an easy task, as he had to accomplish it without a mirror. He managed it though, but by touch, and felt that he had probably done a reasonable enough job under the circumstances. After this, he attempted to go back to sleep again, hoping it would stop him from dwelling once again on his thoughts and fears. Unfortunately, as he had spent so much of the previous day asleep, he found it difficult to drift off, and only succeeded in having a very light doze.

Lunch that day consisted of bread and cheese, which arrived at noon. This was a much larger, tastier portion than he'd expected. Daniel had barely finished eating when the door unexpectedly opened. Inspector Ryder appeared, along with a constable, who was holding hand and leg cuffs. Inspector Ryder briefly explained to Daniel that they were taking him back to

Great Hadham, in order for him to be formally charged. From there he would be taken to another place, to await his trial. Daniel was then put into the restraints and led from the cell.

As soon as he reached the outside world, the first thing that struck him was that the icy wind had now dropped, and it was several degrees warmer than it had been when he arrived on the Monday. It was also evident that at some point that morning, or possibly the day before, there had been a drop of rain, as much of the snow, which had lain on the ground for several days, had now melted.

Parked outside the building was a horse-drawn Black Mariah, an enclosed prisoner's cart, which Daniel was helped up into via some small steps at the back, before being locked into a small cubicle within the carriage. The Mariah had a markedly foreboding presence about it, yet Daniel was relieved that his journey back to Hadham was going to be in this, not in the open cart he'd been taken away in just a few days earlier.

There appeared to be a considerable delay before they moved off, although in reality it was probably no more than five minutes. Daniel was unable to see out and could hear very little sound, certainly no distinct voices. Not knowing what was going on was all quite disconcerting for him. Eventually he heard a sound of what he thought may have been Inspector Ryder's voice, and within seconds the Mariah gave a little jolt, and they began to move off.

Half an hour later they came to a halt. Daniel heard the door opening at the back of the Mariah, and at almost the same time, the tiny cell door was unlocked. The constable appeared in the doorway, beckoning with his hand for Daniel to come out, and led the way down the steps. As Daniel followed behind him, he was able to see over the constable's head. It was a familiar view for him. Instantly recognising that he was outside Gayton and Mott's, the solicitors, in his home village.

Inspector Ryder was standing at the bottom of the steps, and he held Daniel's right arm as he stepped onto the road. The constable took hold of Daniel's left arm as he was escorted into the solicitors' office.

Once inside, he was introduced to the magistrate, Mr R. Dawson Esq. An imposing gentleman of stature, with distinguished features. Daniel recognised him as being the owner of Albury Hall, in a nearby village. Ironically, Daniel had been there only a few months earlier, delivering a cart of hay from the farm at Bromley Hall. Mr Dawson showed no sign of recognition towards Daniel, which came as no surprise to him. For why should a member of the landed gentry have ever remembered a lowly delivery worker?

Mr Dawson was sitting behind a large, dark-mahogany kneehole desk. On top of the desk was a pile of small books, and beside them, a larger book with a plush red leather cover. In front of him were a few sheets of writing paper, the top piece of which was full of large flowing handwriting. On the edge of the desk was a long, beautifully ornate, silvered inkwell set. It was complete with an old quill pen, a dip pen, and a new, expensive-looking, gold-tipped fountain pen.

As Daniel was being led in, he had spotted a man sitting on a small wooden chair at the back of the room, who was writing down something in a notebook. Daniel had seen him in the village a few times before. He didn't know for sure, but he believed the man to be a reporter from the local Hertfordshire newspaper.

Mr Mott, the partner at the solicitors' firm, was also present, along with Constable Newland, Mr Knight, and another man whom he had never seen before. He assumed this was the owner of the stack – if not, he knew he would soon find out.

All of a sudden Daniel began feeling rather hot and could sense his cheeks reddening, as a deep wave of embarrassment spread over his face. Even so, he still felt no sense of shame or remorse regarding the act which had brought him to this place. Daniel stood in front of the desk with his head bowed, trying not to make eye contact with Mr Dawson, or anyone else.

Mr Dawson tapped hard on his desk in order to gain the attention of all in the room. Then in a refined accent said, 'Daniel Phillips, you are here today being charged with wilfully setting a stack on fire. The stack being the property of Mr Snow of Puckeridge. The barley stack was the produce of thirteen and a half acres. Valued at one hundred and fifty shillings.'

Still with his head lowered, Daniel was gently moved to the side by Inspector Ryder, allowing space at the front of the desk for the gentleman, who Daniel thought may have been the owner of the stack, to come forward. It quickly transpired that he was indeed Mr Snow, who proceeded to confirm what Mr Dawson had just stated regarding his ownership of the barley stack, before returning to the side of the room.

Constable Newland then made his way to the front of the desk, looking at Daniel as he went. Daniel, still with his head lowered, raised his eyes upwards, making eye contact with him. With his lips tightly shut, he gave an apologetic half-smile. Constable Newland closed his eyes briefly and slowly turned his head towards Mr Dawson, in what appeared to be an expression of disgust as to what Daniel had done.

Mr Dawson asked Constable Newland to state all of the evidence he had managed to gather so far, which had given him reason to arrest Daniel. At this request, Constable Newland took out a familiar-looking notebook from his top pocket and proceeded to read from both that and a larger police journal which he had been holding under his arm.

As he began reading out his official account of Monday's incident, along with the conversations which had taken place between the two of them, the enormity of Daniel's actions became even clearer to him. There had been moments over the past few days when he'd thought he understood the fullness of this, but clearly that wasn't the case.

Daniel stood with his head still bowed, in a daze. He could hear different voices around him, each speaking in turn, yet he was not hearing any of the words they were uttering, only the tone of their voices.

After a while, he suddenly became conscious of a silence in the room which brought him out of the state he was in. At the same time he felt Inspector Ryder grip his upper arm, moving him towards the front of the desk again. For the first time Daniel looked up, focusing on Mr Dawson sitting before him.

'Daniel Phillips, how do you plead to this charge, guilty or not guilty?'

Daniel knew it was pointless pleading his innocence. It was impossible to undo what he had done, and retracting his previous confession would have been futile, even if he had wanted to. Which he didn't.

He peered over Mr Dawson's head, to the window behind him. He could see that it was now raining, heavily at that. Pleasant thoughts returned to him on how warm and sunny the weather was meant to be in Australia, reaffirming his desire to make his dream come true of having a better life out there one day.

Daniel could tell he was now smiling from ear to ear, which was most certainly not an appropriate reaction to be showing in the environment he was now in. He straightened his mouth at once, looking back towards Mr Dawson.

'I'm guilty, sir, guilty.'

Mr Dawson tidied up the papers in front of him, placed the fountain pen carefully down on top of them, and said, 'In that case, Daniel Phillips, you are to be fully committed for trial at the next assizes. Which is due to be held in two months' time.'

Almost before Daniel knew what was happening to him, he was whisked out of the office by Inspector Ryder and the other constable, who put him back into the small cell inside the Mariah. He was unable to see out, but as they moved off he was sure, judging by the motions of the vehicle, that instead of turning around, heading back towards Stortford, they were travelling in the opposite direction, down the high street. This being the case, it meant that before too long he would be going past the crossroads in the village, within sight of his home.

His heart gave a flutter, knowing there could be a chance of getting one last glimpse of his home or possibly even see his mother. That was if he could manage to find a way to see out. He pressed his face against the side of the cart, desperately hoping to find a small crack, or even just a pinhole in the slats. Frustratingly, his attempts were fruitless. In an explosion of anger, he banged his fists on the walls of the Mariah. A shot of pain went through one of his knuckles, telling him in no uncertain terms that this was not going to help the situation.

Daniel settled back down. Now with a calmer mind, he figured that he should try once again to work out his whereabouts in the village by sensing the motions of the vehicle. It seemed, by the way he had been tilting towards the door at the back, that they had been going up a steep incline in the road. Then, judging by the quickening of the horses' hooves, and that he was now clearly leaning towards the front, it was obvious they were going downhill. This being the case, he was certain that he was now heading down Tower Hill, therefore was about to pass through Hadham Cross, the area of the village where he lived.

Yet again, a wave of frustration came over him. He became exceedingly agitated in his movements, knowing that unless he was able to see out of the vehicle within a few seconds, he was unlikely ever to get the chance to see his home again. He frantically scanned the inside walls of the cell, looking for a pinprick of light which could give him the opportunity for a final glimpse of home, but all his efforts were still to no avail.

A few minutes later his restlessness began to ease, as he began to accept the fact that by now they must have left the village.

Having been so near to his home, yet unable to view it, had so disturbed him that he had ceased attempting to guess his whereabouts. So, out of curiosity, he once again began trying to sense the movements of the vehicle, matching this with what he knew of the roads surrounding the village. Annoyingly, nothing seemed to fit. An awful feeling of disorientation began swirling around his mind. He slumped forward, sticking his fingers in his ears, attempting to silence the crunching sound which was coming from the wheels of the Mariah as it trundled along the road.

With the sound now muffled, he tried coming to terms with the fact that he may never get the chance to return to the village or see his mother and the rest of his family ever again. At first this thought almost brought him to tears, but as the first drops began to fill his eyes, his emotions swung in the other direction, feeling quite indifferent to the notion.

It was almost an hour later before it dawned on him that he didn't know where he was being taken. He remembered that on the day of his arrest, Constable Newland had mentioned the possibility of going to Hertford Gaol, but he hadn't been told anything since. At least he didn't think he had, having spent most of his time at the solicitors' in an incoherent haze. If something had been said, he certainly hadn't taken it in.

As he was dwelling on this, the Mariah slowed down, coming to a halt. The door opened, with the constable beckoning for Daniel to get out. He complied, being helped down the steps by Inspector Ryder.

In front of him was a large building. Although Daniel had never set eyes on a prison before, he could tell, without any doubt, it clearly was such a place.

'Where are we, Inspector?' enquired Daniel.

'Hertford Gaol,' he replied, leading him towards the entrance.

Daniel knew there were two gaols in Hertford, one

in the middle of town, the other, a newer one, on the outskirts of the town. This was clearly the gaol outside the town.

It wasn't long before Daniel found himself going through the humiliating assessment process. An unpleasant experience, which he had not at all been prepared for. Once this had been completed, he was taken off to a cell. This was about eight feet by five feet, and it was to be his home for twenty-three hours a day, for the next eight weeks. It came complete with a bucket toilet, a small table with a large open Bible on it, a stool, and an iron bed fixed to the wall. Hanging on the wall was a list of prison rules. Every one of which began with: 'All prisoners shall...' and ended with: '...shall be severely punished'.

The first two weeks seemed to go by relatively quickly, and there were times when he felt as if he was at the beginning of an exciting adventure, a sort of grand tour, the likes of which only the very wealthy would go on. Only not with the luxurious accommodation and means of travel that such folk would have enjoyed.

One day, during the third week of his confinement, his mother was permitted to visit him. To begin with, the atmosphere between them was extremely tense. Neither quite knowing what to say to the other. Or rather, they knew what they wanted to say but didn't know how to say it. Eventually though, and through tears from them both, his mother made it clear to him how much she loved him. However, she didn't hide the hurt caused by what he had done to her and the rest of his family.

This revelation hit Daniel hard. From then on every day dragged slowly by, the like of which he'd never experienced before, and left him feeling incredibly isolated and lonely.

CHAPTER 9

Trial and Prison

Wednesday, 2 March 1864

The Lent Assizes were opened by Sir F.J. Pollock Esq. at Shire Hall, in the county town of Hertford.

After the formalities had been completed, he was accompanied by the High Sheriff and a number of other dignitaries on the short walk to All Saints Church. Here a short service, which always preceded a forthcoming trial, took place. Following the service, they all retired until the following day, when twenty-two men of the grand jury, respected local gentlemen and landowners, were sworn in. Then the trials of prisoners commenced.

The previous Sunday, Daniel had been forewarned by the prison's religious instructor that the Lent Assizes would be getting underway that week. Unfortunately, Daniel hadn't thought to ask which day his case was expected to be heard, so every morning, no sooner were his eyes open than he began wondering what that day was going to bring forth.

This was a challenging feeling for him to cope with, as over the past eight weeks he had become accustomed to living with the same daily routine. Day after day he would be locked inside his cell, with the only breaks in monotony being meal times and an hour's exercise. This involved walking in a circle around the courtyard in all weathers. He would always be accompanied by several other prisoners, all of them in chains, and were forbidden to communicate with each other in any way. Although there was one warder who appeared to deliberately turn a blind eye when prisoners passed near to where he was standing. Even though this enabled Daniel to exchange the odd whispered word with whoever was in front of or behind him, it had to be done in a very discreet manner.

It wasn't until the Friday morning of the trial that Daniel, along with two other prisoners, was taken from the prison and driven to Shire Hall. Due to him having already pleaded guilty and having made no request since to change his plea, his case was considered in a very short time by the grand jury. It came as no surprise to him to receive the mandatory sentence set out for his crime: '...to be kept for seven years in penal servitude'.

In passing sentence, the judge had made no reference to him being transported from these shores, so as Daniel climbed down from the dock, he had a momentary panic, fearing the judge had decided not to 'reward' him in granting his desire. However, by the time he reached the bottom step, he'd realised that the judge had no need to say this, as he'd been sentenced for one of the crimes punishable by transportation.

Later that day, Daniel was returned to Hertford Gaol, where he spent the night for the last time. As he lay on his bunk, he began thinking about some of the other prisoners whom he had been with in the holding area of the court. Especially the ones who had been issued with the same sentence as himself, but who had been displaying signs of great distress from the moment they came down from the dock.

As for himself, he had left court with a peculiar feeling of contentment, feeling rather unsympathetic towards the others around him who were in such turmoil. But now, knowing they would be in their cells, doing nothing other than dwelling on their punishments and facing a long sleepless night ahead, Daniel began to feel pity for them. Yet he still had no feeling of guilt for what he'd just been convicted of.

Full of contentment, he soon drifted off to sleep.

***

The following day Daniel was taken on the long journey to Aylesbury Gaol, where he experienced the toughest few weeks of his life that he had ever encountered ... so far.

On arrival, he went through a few formalities before being taken off to a side room where he had his hair heavily cropped. It was so close that it came complete with four nicks. The first one caused him to give a small yelp, although this was more from surprise than pain. Not wanting to appear unmanly, he was able to react to the other three nicks with no more than a small flinch. Following this, he was ordered into a bath of foul-smelling water, which he assumed was some kind of disinfectant. These things over, he was then issued with his prison uniform. A coarse light-coloured jacket, grey trousers, and a square pillbox cap.

Having put on his new attire, he was marched off to his new cell. This was much the same size as the one in Hertford, complete with similar accessories, except for two things. One of these being the bed. In Hertford Gaol, this had been a rather lumpy stuffed mattress. But here in Aylesbury, there was no such luxury to be enjoyed. His mattress was simply a few wooden boards to lie on.

That night Daniel was glad that his previous night's sleep had been a good one, as he was about to have one of the most uncomfortable sleepless nights of his life. He feared that he would never get a good night's sleep again, at least not while in prison. However, this proved not to be the case, as the following night he fell asleep without any effort. Although this was solely down to the things he had endured during the day and the lack of sleep from the night before.

On Daniel's first full day in Aylesbury, he was introduced to the forced daily regime of hard labour, which came as a massive shock to him. Many times over the past few months he had thought about what life in gaol would be like. He had heard stories in the past, both hearsay and from those who had experienced prison first-hand, but things were now turning out to be far more punishing than anything he had ever previously contemplated.

Here in Aylesbury there was something in his cell which had been absent from his cell in Hertford. This was 'the crank'. A hugely unwelcome addition, which he was forced to operate every day. The crank was a mechanical box, with a handle on one side and a small counter which showed how many times the handle had been turned. When the handle was turned, it would move a series of cogs, which in turn rotated some paddles that were on the inside of the box. This alone was something not to be relished, but the box also contained sand, thus making the revolving of the handle an immensely more difficult task.

In addition to this contraption was a warder, who would be constantly looking in or silently watching on for long periods of time. If he was in a bad mood that day, or had simply taken a disliking to a prisoner, then he would alter the screws on the box. This added yet another level of difficulty with turning the handle. Because of this, Daniel soon understood why the prison warders were known by the inmates as 'screws'.

Every morning Daniel would be required to turn the handle two thousand times before he was allowed to have any breakfast. After breakfast he would be required to turn it three thousand times in order to earn his lunch, and afterwards, three thousand more turns to be rewarded with supper. But this wasn't the end of it.

Another two thousand turns had to be made before he was allowed to retire to his bed for the night.

This punishment was not only physically painful for his arms and joints, but by the end of the first day he was suffering from two very nasty blisters. One on his forefinger and another much larger one on the palm of his hand, which had also burst. These, along with another one gained the following day, made things painfully slow.

The mind-numbing monotony of being engaged on the crank was also exceptionally hard for Daniel to cope with. Especially during the first week of his incarceration. For the majority of this time, his thoughts mainly revolved around two things in particular. One, which had distressed him ever since his arrest, was what thoughts his mother and family were probably having towards him. The other was not knowing how much longer he would be able to endure this daily torture.

There were some mornings when, as soon his eyes opened, he would begin having serious doubts as to whether he would make it until the end of that day and still be of sound mind. Fortunately, after just a few days, he figured that the best thing to do would be to either make his mind go blank and not think about anything at all, or do the opposite and let his imagination wander way off into the future. He found the latter most helpful. Indeed, there were times when his daydreaming about a future life in the warmth and freedom of Australia seemed so real it was as if he had already arrived.

CHAPTER 10

Off to Chatham

To Daniel's immense relief, his time in Aylesbury Gaol lasted less than three weeks. On the twenty-second of March he, along with four other prisoners, were taken by horse-drawn Mariah to London. There, they were loaded into a small carriage at the back of a train, in order to be taken to St Mary's Prison in Chatham, Kent. This was the first time Daniel had been on a steam train, and although he was not looking forward to reaching its destination, he found himself enjoying the journey.

It was mid-afternoon when the train pulled up at the station. Daniel and his fellow prisoners were made to wait in the carriage until all other passengers had left the station before they were escorted from the train and taken to Chatham Prison.

As the main prison building came into view, Daniel scanned the imposing gatehouse with a sense of wonder and admiration at its impressive architecture.

In the middle of the central tower was a giant double wooden door with a portcullis hanging a quarter of the way down from the top. Above this was a large bell tower with a clock face on each of its sides. Having spent all his life living in the country, Daniel was more than a little impressed by the sight, and just as he was thinking it couldn't appear any better, the sun peeped through the clouds, lighting up the clock face.

As the prisoners and their guards were approaching the door, it was opened up by a warder from inside the prison. Daniel turned his head to the side, whispering to the man who was marginally behind him, 'I think I'm gonna like it here!' and with it gave a little chuckle.

'I can assure you, lad, you won't. They'll soon be removing that smile off your face,' came a gruff reply from the convict. He was a lot older than Daniel and seemed to speak with an authority of someone who had probably experienced prison life before.

This jolted Daniel back down to earth, as it registered to him, this wasn't some sort of sightseeing trip, but instead he was about to be confined inside the walls of this building. Also, as the previous few weeks' experience had shown, those in authority would, without any doubt, be doing all they could to stop him from smiling.

I must never let this happen, he thought to himself, and without intending to he blurted out, much too loudly, 'Never.'

'No talking,' shouted one of the escorting guards who was behind him. At the same time he aggressively shoved Daniel through the doorway, causing him to fall to the ground with a thud.

Grabbing the small chain between Daniel's hands, the warder pulled him up with such vigour it caused the cuffs to go partly over his wrists, sending a sharp pain up through his hands to the tips of his fingers.

He screamed out in pain, whilst at the same time attempting to get his feet from underneath himself in order to stand up again. Once upright, he found himself face to face with the prisoner whom he had just spoken to. Nothing was said between them – there didn't need to be, as Daniel could tell exactly what he was thinking: *I told you so.*

Seeing this look from the other prisoner caused a wave of stubbornness to well up from within. Along with it came a determination, telling him that he must never give up on his pursuit of gaining a better life. Whatever might be thrown at him along the way.

Buoyed by this feeling, he raised a smile towards the prisoner, as an outward sign of his defiance. He wasn't sure if the other prisoner was taken in by this, but it made him feel stronger in himself, if only for that brief moment.

Daniel was the first to be taken away to a small side room where he went through a similar process to that which he'd gone through on arrival at Hertford and Aylesbury Gaol. Even though he was prepared for it, he still found this formality –especially the body search – uncomfortably embarrassing.

Having completed all the formalities, he was led away to the main prison block. This was a massive structure of walkways, stairs, and iron railings, leading to blocks of cells from floor to roof.

Daniel was taken up the first flight of stairs and along the landing. About halfway along the warder stopped, unlocked one of the cell doors, and pointing towards it, said with a stern tone, 'Inside.'

Without hesitation Daniel did as he was told.

On entering the cell he noted something that made him give a massive sigh of relief. Although the cell didn't look too dissimilar to the one at Aylesbury, there was one major thing missing … the crank. The relief at its absence only lasted a split second though, as he was struck with the dreaded thought that this piece of apparatus was missing because he'd now be facing the treadwheel instead. Judging from the secret whispered tales he had heard from inmates at Aylesbury, this was a far more difficult and dangerous punishment to encounter.

The warder handed Daniel a copy of the prison's rules, even though most had been relayed to him on arrival, then he left, banging the door firmly behind him, still without saying a word.

A short time later the door opened, and Daniel was handed a bowl of gruel, a chunk of bread, and mug of tea. Sitting down on the floor to eat it, he began casting his mind back to that tasty rabbit stew, which he had enjoyed with Levi a few months earlier. He longed to have that taste in his mouth once again and, at that moment, would have given anything to exchange his gruel for a taste of rabbit stew. Unfortunately, even with all the wishing in the world, he knew this delight would not be coming his way for many years.

Halfway through eating he paused, with a spoonful of gruel touching his lips. It had suddenly dawned on him that at no point had he been told, or even given a clue, as to how long he'd be locked away in this place. He hoped it would only be for a few days or at most a few weeks. But worryingly, the chaplain in Aylesbury Gaol had mentioned it could possibly be several months. It all depended on when the next departure of a convict ship was planned for, and how many convicts were already in line for this journey to the other side of the world.

Daniel stared blankly towards the door, becoming overwhelmed with a sensation the like of which he'd never experienced before. It was an awful claustrophobic feeling, as if the walls of his cell were closing in on him. His heart began palpitating, he found himself struggling to breathe, and he began to panic.

He put the spoonful of gruel into his mouth and swallowed, but instead of going straight down, it became lodged in his throat. He made several attempts to swallow, but failing to dislodge it, he began to choke violently. Instinctively grabbing the mug of tea, he took a small mouthful and somehow managed to swallow enough to wash it down.

Daniel breathed a sigh of relief, but the relief was short-lived, as a deep wave of fear hit him regarding the uncertainty of what his future might hold. He put his head in his hands and attempted to breathe slowly, concentrating on this action in the hope it would help stifle the tears which were now filling his eyes.

I mustn't lose control, I must try to think of something good in all this, he thought to himself.

At once he sat upright, as an idea from nowhere sprang to mind. An idea which he felt sure could be of help to him, not only in this precise moment of distress, but for the duration of his sentence. He figured that the best way forward was to refrain from calling his cell, a cell. From now on he would regard it as a room, his own room. A room that, for the first time in his life, wouldn't need to be shared with anyone else.

Surveying his new room, the walls were now back in place, and once again he was breathing with ease. Daniel smiled to himself. *Wow, I now have my very own room.*

Peering into his bowl of gruel, he knew there was no use in pretending here. Its texture and tastelessness was never going to be a match for the rabbit stew or his mother's home cooking. Even so, he decided to look on the bright side, knowing that at least he could be assured of receiving food three times a day. An assurance that he'd not had the pleasure of for a long time.

Still fresh with the memory of that last mouthful of gruel he'd taken, he gingerly took another spoonful. This time it went down with ease, and somehow it had developed a little more taste too.

CHAPTER 11

Prison Life

On his first full day at Chatham, Daniel was awoken by the early sound of the 5 a.m. bell ringing throughout the prison. This was accompanied by warders noisily going along the prison walkways, banging on each cell door and opening the small viewing hatch, making sure all prisoners were still inside, and alive.

Daniel lay on his bed, staring up at the ceiling, wondering what that first full day would be bringing his way. Whatever it was, he was fairly sure that it would follow a similar patten to the ones which he had gone through in Aylesbury Gaol. Although with no crank in sight, he would probably be spending the day on and off the treadwheel instead.

Daniel got up, packed his bed away, as had been instructed on arrival, then made himself as comfortable as he could on the floor, while constantly glancing towards the door in anticipation of its opening. He could hear the sounds of the prisoners and warders, going back and forth along the landing. Each time any sound appeared to be approaching his door, he watched expectantly for it to open, and to be led away to endure the delights of the wheel. But time continued to pass by without anything happening. In fact it was another two hours before any movement came from the door. When it did, a trustee prisoner appeared, holding a tray. He took one step inside, placed the tray on the floor, pushed it slightly forward, saying, 'Breakfast.'

Unsurprisingly, the tray held the usual bread, gruel, and tea. Without saying anything else, the man left as suddenly as he had appeared, giving Daniel no chance of saying anything to him.

From his experiences over the past few weeks, he knew that a reply was unlikely to be forthcoming anyway. Nevertheless, he wasn't put off from trying if opportunities arose. Occasionally his attempts to exchange a few snatched words with the person serving could be rewarded, but he was acutely aware these times would always be a rarity. The trustee would not only need to be out of earshot of any warder, but eyeshot too. For if a warder was to even suspect the trustee was attempting to converse with a prisoner, it would inevitably mean his loss of this position, and probably a further punishment on top of that.

Daniel was still eating his breakfast when he heard the sound of a key unlocking the door. In came a stocky, well-built warder, who slammed the door shut behind him.

'Stand up, Phillips,' he ordered. Even though he could see that Daniel was already on his way up.

'What's going to happen today, sir?' enquired Daniel with trepidation in his voice.

'That depends on whether you intend to behave or not ... Misbehave and you'll find yourself spending many days locked in heavy chains in a dark cell below. And with no more than bread and water for sustenance. Or, if you choose to be very disruptive, there is always a good floggin' until you pass out.' He paused briefly to allow this warning to sink in. Although this wasn't really needed, as the warning had already registered, sending Daniel's heart thumping with fear. The warder continued, 'However, if you conform, you'll be able to take in some of the lovely fresh air at the dockyard, on a working party. Breaking up and moving rocks for shoring up the dockside is today's pleasure. But be warned, try to escape and you will suffer both the other fates.'

'No, I won't be trying to escape, sir. I don't want to escape at all,' replied Daniel.

'Right, no more talking, follow me,' snapped the warder, taking no notice of Daniel's reply.

Needing no more incentive, Daniel did as he was told.

He had only taken a few steps along the landing when he noticed that something rather significant was missing from his time spent in Aylesbury Gaol. He had no longer been forced to wear a hood over his face while out of his cell.

During his time in Aylesbury Gaol, he would only

be let out of his cell once a day, for an hour of exercise. That was apart from a Sunday, when the addition of a short service in the chapel was included. Once inside the chapel, the prisoners' hoods were removed, then they were made to sit in small, individual cubicles. This was designed to prohibit any chance of conversing or passing anything they shouldn't on to other convicts.

Wearing the hood was a stifling, disorientating experience. But now, every step that Daniel was taking along the landing gave him an increasing feeling of optimism. Looking around, he could see several prisoners on the other landings, and ground floor. These men were hoodless too. This gave him the final bit of evidence needed. He was now certain it was not simply an oversight. Clearly the hood was not part of the system here at Chatham Gaol.

During his introduction to the establishment, and from having read the rules, Daniel was left in no doubt that things were still going to be tough here. It had been made abundantly clear from the start that conversing with other prisoners was, on the whole, forbidden. Only in certain circumstances was talking permitted, mainly restricted to asking or answering questions in connection with the task he was involved in. The only other occasion he could talk with another prisoner was if he could be absolutely certain of not getting caught.

The dockyard was only a short walk from the prison, and the first thing which struck him as he was being led outside to join a working party was the weather. It was a bright, sunny spring morning, and even though he had no idea how hard the labour was going to be that day, he found himself looking forward to spending this day in the open air.

Having spent all of his working life outside, this was something he had missed since his confinement. Indeed, at no point while he'd been evaluating the downsides of life in gaol, had he actually considered this loss.

At Chatham, the majority of Daniel's working days were spent working around the docks. This was, physically, extremely demanding work. Especially when tasked with such jobs as the breaking up and moving of rocks, as was given to him on his first day.

Along with this work came blisters, cuts, bruises, and muscle strains. None of which were looked on by the authorities as good enough reasons to be permitted to have a day or two back in the cells to recover. Only with severe cases would the gaol's doctor recommend this, and even then another task was usually found, or even made up, which was able to be done in such a way that it didn't affect the injury.

When the weather was pleasant, it always gave Daniel the extra boost needed to help him get through the day. However, work was carried out in all weathers, come rain or shine. Along with the ever watchful eyes of the prison guards, ensuring there was little, if any, opportunity to rest or shirk.

Daniel didn't spend his entire time labouring

outside. There were also indoor assignments too. He was often made to undertake tasks such as picking oakum. This was not only an immensely boring job, it also made the tips of his fingers extremely painful and sore. If he was engaged on this job, and was not sitting on one of the front or outer benches where he could be easily spotted by a warder, he was sometimes able to use a small piece of pointed stick, or slither of flint, to assist in this task. But he had to be careful of other prisoners spotting this too. As they could be tempted to snitch, in the hope of gaining a little favour from a warder at a later date. Not that it was very likely, but he still had to have his wits about him.

Daniel also noted that he would rarely be given an indoor job if the weather was wet or very cold. He was never too sure if this was simply coincidence or not, but he had a strong suspicion it wasn't.

The food at Chatham varied little week to week, although weekends often had a slight variation to them. This was not only welcomed in the obvious way, it also helped him to keep track of which day of the week it was. The meals usually consisted of oatmeal gruel, potatoes, bread, with the occasional serving of meat, fish, and cheese. There were extra rations to be had, with things such as soup, beef-suet pudding, and cocoa. Usually this was only in conjunction with having been carrying out hard labour that day. On the whole the food was a bland, tasteless menu. Yet he was constantly comforted with the assurance that he would at least be getting food three or four times a day.

It wasn't just the physical side of the work he found tough. It was also the lack of being able to converse freely with others, and the monotony of the prison's repetitive daily structure.

Gradually all these things combined and began taking their toll on Daniel's health. He started suffering from ever increasing periods when waves of darkness would shroud his mind. Some days he became so low in spirit he was unable to see any end to it all. He often became convinced that he'd never live long enough to experience life outside of the prison, let alone reach his ultimate dream.

One of the biggest worries he struggled with had been brought on by something he'd been told shortly after arriving at Chatham.

Daniel had been working with three other convicts near the docks, unloading rocks from a cart. The nearest guard was some way off, clearly more interested in talking to a fellow guard than keeping a close eye on the prisoners. So, not wanting to let this opportunity pass them by, they were able to spend several minutes talking to each other, albeit very discreetly.

While chatting, Daniel had briefly explained to them his crime, or misdemeanour as he saw it, and why he had committed the act. In response, one of the prisoners told him something which cast a huge cloud of doubt as to whether he would ever get the chance to achieve his dream. The prisoner told Daniel that he had previously been in the employment of an MP, working on his large estate in the West Country. Because of his position there, he would often hear snippets of information regarding the various goings on in government. This was mainly gleaned from fellow members of staff having overheard chatter from members of the MP's family, but it was usually fairly close to the truth.

One such piece of news was that debates had been going on in Parliament, suggesting that the transportation of convicts would soon be coming to an end. Daniel wasn't completely sure if the prisoner had made this up on the spur of the moment, as some kind of bad joke, or if he had been telling the truth. But he hadn't come across as the kind of person who would do such a thing, so this news soon began causing Daniel a great deal of additional distress.

In view of this news, and the increasing worry caused, Daniel decided it was time to find out the truth of the situation. So when the prison's religious instructor was next on his rounds, he questioned him about this rumour. To his horror, this story was confirmed, creating an even greater degree of havoc within his mind.

Daniel understood that most prisoners would be delighted with this news. So, being the sort of person he was, whenever possible he'd share it with others. But for himself, it meant that all he had gone through, and put his family through, would have been for nothing. He would end up having to spend the whole seven years of his sentence doing hard labour in England. Then, at the end of his sentence, he would be worse off than before. Try as he might, to put this bleak news to the back of his mind was all but impossible.

Time went on. Weeks turned into months, then into years. There were many times when waves of deep depression came over him, dragging him down into the depths of despair. His smile, which had been noted early on by his fellow inmates as one which could appear without much encouragement, had been absent for some time, no matter what amusing things were said or had occurred.

The prison's religious instructor made regular visits to Daniel, which were much welcomed by him, as it was the only opportunity to talk freely and openly with another human being.

Daniel recognised that being able to offload all the daily struggles and worries he was encountering was crucial in keeping him from completely losing his mind.

Another reason he always appreciated these visits was that it gave him the chance to explore his ever developing interest in God. He had now begun praying more often. Interestingly, there had been times when he had been left with a strange sort of peaceful feeling inside, which he found hard to comprehend.

There had also been occasions when a prayer he had made, regarding a problem or issue he had been encountering, had been readily resolved, in quite unexpected ways. Something he found rather fascinating.

A few weeks after Daniel had arrived at Chatham, he had been warned by fellow prisoner that part of the religious instructor's job was to keep reports on all the prisoners. These reports would often be relayed back to the governor of the gaol.

On receiving this information, Daniel immediately understood the need to be highly cautious of anything that he talked about. He also wished he'd known about this situation beforehand. This was because he'd already explained to the religious instructor, in some detail, his reasoning for committing the act. Also, that he still believed his firing of the stack in order to get a better life for himself in Australia wasn't such a terrible thing to have done. In fact, in his own eyes, he was convinced that it didn't really make him such a bad man as the rest of society now made him out to be.

Two years had now passed since he struck those matches up at Notley Wells. Finding himself still at Chatham Gaol had brought Daniel to the conclusion that, by having openly spoken about his motives, along with his lack of remorse, was definitely the wrong thing to have done. He became convinced that he was being deliberately kept in gaol until the transportation programme had finally come to an end, to ensure he would never receive any benefit from what people saw as his 'crime'.

This situation was now deeply affecting him,

adding to the increasing periods of being plunged into deep waves of depression. Another trigger, which would often cause him to suffer dark moments of mind, was the fact that he had not heard anything from his mother or other family members during those past two years.

On his arrival at Chatham Gaol, Daniel had been permitted to write to his mother, informing her of his whereabouts. She was barely able to read or write, so he knew she wouldn't have understood a great deal of what he had written. On the other hand, his stepfather was a very able man, as were his brothers and sister, so Daniel felt sure that one of them would have read it to her. He had also been hoping for a reply which would include some form of words of forgiveness from his mother towards him.

Sadly, no reply ever came. He felt certain that he'd been completely shunned by his family and would never be welcomed back by them, or anyone from his village, ever again.

On one particular night, all these negative thoughts surrounding the situation he was in came together at once, sending him plummeting down to the lowest point he'd ever reached. As he was agonising over the helplessness of the situation in the dark ravine of his mind, he came to the conclusion that all the physical and mental suffering was now too much to bear. He was now certain, beyond any doubt, that his plan for achieving a better life was over. As a result of the multitude of things stacked against him, he had come to the end of the road, unable to face any more turmoil or suffering in his life.

With this conclusion in mind, he made a pledge to himself. The following morning, when working near the dockside, he was going to break away from the rest of the gang and throw himself into the water. As he was unable to swim, he knew his life's suffering would be over with in no time at all.

Daniel hardly slept that night, just occasionally dozing. In the morning, as he was being escorted from his cell, he was still full of determination to carry out his plan. Nothing, or nobody, was going to be able to stop him now. He was going to end it all.

There was, however, one thing he hadn't accounted for. On that particular morning, the rota had been changed. Instead of being taken to the dockyard to work, he was taken off to one of the workshops inside the gaol compound. Although this wasn't an unusual occurrence, he hadn't anticipated it occurring on that particular morning.

Ironically, it was an extremely dull, wet morning, too. On any other day he would have been enormously grateful to be given the chance of working inside, but not on this day. The change of work place had not only scuppered his plan, it made him even more depressed than the night before, and on more than one occasion a number of uncontrollable tears trickled down his face.

The workshop was a very dark, lonely place that morning, leaving him with a feeling as if he was in a bubble, completely removed from everything around him.

Several times warders had spoken to him, giving instructions or orders, but worryingly, however simple they were, he struggled to understand even the simplest task given to him, let alone accomplish it.

It was at midday that something happened which dramatically changed the whole situation for him.

Daniel and the other convicts in the workshop were all sitting in a circle, eating dinner with the usual enforced silence, when suddenly, and without any warning, the dark rain clouds parted, making the room become increasingly lighter and lighter. This was soon followed by a bright beam of sunlight bursting through a window from behind him. It seemed to land in the middle of the circle where he was sitting. He turned his head to see the source of this beam. In doing so, his eyes caught sight of a window that was high up near the ceiling, in front of him. Looking beyond the glass, he could see the roof of a nearby building. Above this, he beheld the most beautiful sight he had seen since his sentence had begun. It was the curve of a large, beautiful, double rainbow.

As he studied it, his memory passed back to a conversation which had taken place many years previously, and until now he had forgotten all about.

It was at some point during his childhood, during an afternoon stroll with his mother, when they came across a small group of Irish navvies, who were heading towards Devon, seeking work on a new railway line. While his mother was talking to them, Daniel spotted a rainbow above a woodland in the distance. Daniel remembered one of the men telling him that there would now be a large pot of gold sitting at the end of the rainbow.

Daniel pestered his mother all the way home, trying to persuade her to take him over to the woods, unable to understand why she did not want to go.

Now, as an adult, he obviously knew this was no more than a tale, without any truth in it whatsoever. But even so, in seeing this glorious rainbow in front of him, a new wave of hope began to fill his innermost being.

It had been many months since he had felt so encouraged. 'I mustn't give up, I must keep going,' he muttered to himself. 'While I'm still alive, there's still a chance that I'll make it to the end of the rainbow ... Australia ... and I might even find some of its gold.'

'What's that stupid smile for?' called out one of the warders.

All eyes in the room shot towards the warder in a flash. Daniel automatically knew it was himself that was being addressed, and he hastily stuffed a large piece of bread into his mouth, hoping to disguise the big smile which had spread from ear to ear.

As he was struggling to chew the bread, it dawned on him that lately his smile had become no more than a distant memory. How he'd allowed that to happen he wasn't sure, but right now he didn't care. The important thing was he now knew it was back again, and that his dream was still alive too. Indeed, not only was his dream still alive, but so was he.

CHAPTER 12

Leaving Land

Thursday, 6 September 1866

D aniel had risen from his bed before the first morning bell had sounded. By the time it rang, he had already folded his bed away and was ready and waiting for the daily routine to begin: the unlocking of his cell door, and then he would be off to commence his first work session of the day.

Like every day, he could hear other cell doors being opened before his own was reached. He could also hear various sounds coming from other prisoners and warders making their way along the landing, but curiously all footsteps bypassed his own cell door, without any attempt to open it. Eventually he became tired of standing, waiting, so he flopped down on the floor, with his back against the door.

Two hours later, having got up several times to stretch his legs, he was back down on the floor again, whistling to himself to help pass the time. He was whistling quietly so as not to be heard from the other side of the door, but loud enough to help relieve the boredom.

Somehow, either because of his whistling or boredom, he'd become distracted enough to miss the sound of footsteps, which had moved along the landing and had come to a halt by his cell door. The door opened. 'Breakfast,' came the call from the warder who entered, shoving the food in front of Daniel before leaving. Daniel was perplexed by what was happening, or more to the point, what was not happening. Over the past two years, each day had differed little from the day before. It was the same old daily routine, not only done by the clock, but tedious like the ticking of a clock. Apart from on a Sunday, with its religious service.

But today was a Thursday, and something was very clearly different about it. He was still stuck in his cell, and unable to come up with any reasonable explanation as to why.

Daniel got up and took his breakfast over to the small table in his cell. While eating, he tried again to fathom out why the routine had changed. Perhaps they had simply forgotten him. Or maybe a warder or fellow prisoner had reported him for doing something wrong, and he was going to be taken off to the governor's office. Although he couldn't think of anything that he had knowingly done wrong. He was fairly confident he'd not bent or broken any rules, but he knew that it wouldn't have been the first time a disgruntled prisoner, or even a warder, had made something up against a prisoner to get even with them or gain a little favour with the governor.

Daniel finished his breakfast and continued waiting for something to happen.

At around ten o'clock, he heard a key turning in the lock. He watched as the cell door opened and two warders entered. One was carrying a pair of leg irons, the other a set of wrist cuffs. Daniel got to his feet, fearing what impending situation was about to unfold. He stared at the two warders, waiting for an instruction, but none came. One of the warders was giving an ominous, knowing smirk, which had the desired effect of adding to the fear Daniel was already feeling.

What if he really had been unjustly accused of something? Was he about to be flogged?

Daniel went to enquire as to why the warders were there, but his mouth had now completely dried up. He managed to make a little saliva in his mouth, which seemed to do the trick, helping him swallow. With a slight quiver in his voice, he was able to get a few words out.

'What's happening, sir?'

'You've just had your last night in here ... You're being transported,' replied the smirking warder.

Although Daniel heard what the warder had said, he couldn't believe he'd heard correctly.

'Sorry, what did you say, sir? Am I really going?'

'Yeah,' stated the warder. 'Now, no struggling, these leg irons will be going on you even if we have to use force.'

Daniel stood passively while he was being shackled. His thoughts had flown back to that memorable day in the workshop when his lost hope had been dramatically rejuvenated by the uplifting vision of a rainbow.

He realised his sentence was barely halfway through, so he would certainly be suffering many more tough times ahead. Even so, he was now feeling happy with himself. Happy that he'd managed to survive this far, but more importantly, that all his hopes and dreams of leaving these shores one day, which he'd been harbouring for such a long time and on occasions had all but vanished, were now very much alive. He really was continuing on the journey towards his dream.

The warder who had been securing the leg irons stood up, only to see Daniel's beaming smile.

'I dunno what you are smiling for, fella. You won't be smiling soon, when you leave these shores for good.'

On hearing these words, Daniel's memory flashed back again. This time, to the incident which had occurred on his arrival at the gaol. It was when a convict had warned him that he would soon have the smile removed from his face. This warning was immediately followed up by a guard knocking him to the floor.

But now, having spent over two years in gaol, he was not only still standing, he was also still smiling.

Daniel gave a sideways grin, sniggering out loud. The warder pushed Daniel heavily in the small of his back, towards the door. He stumbled, falling onto his knees, yet somehow managed to get himself back up in one movement by putting his hands around the edge of the door to help. His knee was a little painful from the fall, but not wanting the warders to have pleasure in seeing his pain, he gritted his teeth and shuffled out of the cell. With one warder in front of him, the other behind.

Oh well, I'm leaving the same way as I came in! he thought while raising an ironic grin.

Daniel was taken out of the cell block and into the gaol's parade ground for the last time. Around forty other convicts were already there, chained together in small groups of around ten men. Daniel was led over to where a group of five men were standing. Then, firmly and securely, he was chain-linked to them.

Another warder was standing close by, ensuring all convicts were waiting in silence and unable to disrupt the ongoing process in any way.

Standing with nothing else to do, Daniel began counting the ever growing number of men being assembled. Even though the men were being chained in small groups, counting was not easy, as there were a large number of guards on hand who were constantly moving back and forth around the yard.

Towards the far side of the yard, Daniel spotted a tall, skinny man. He was clothed in neither prisoner nor guard uniform, but in civilian clothing. He was being escorted around the courtyard by a warder, briefly standing in front of each prisoner in turn, where he was seemingly exchanging a few words with them and occasionally examining various parts of their bodies.

Eventually the man reached Daniel and introduced himself as the Surgeon Superintendent of the prison ship, before enquiring about his health and well-being. Daniel replied he'd never felt finer, so without further ado the man moved on to the next prisoner.

After the prisoners had all been gathered in the courtyard and inspected, the main prison gateway to the outside world was opened. Then, a loud booming voice from a guard informed all in the yard that they were about to be moving out, but each group of prisoners must wait until receiving the order to move from one of the guards beside them.

Gradually, the groups of prisoners were led off, in what seemed to be an orderly, well-practised fashion, with warders guarding each group as they went.

Daniel was near the middle of his group of prisoners. As they began shuffling off, he leaned towards the man in front of him and whispered into his ear, 'There's ninety-eight of us going.'

'Shut up,' came a nervous-sounding reply. Daniel responded with a snort of amusement.

The prisoners slowly made their way out of the prison, then along the road towards the riverside. The sound which came from their shuffling boots, clinking chains, and the occasional groan from someone stumbling, made a peculiar, eerie sound. Daniel could also feel tension in the air from the agitated prisoners around him.

Along with the prison warders, many of whom he knew, there were also a number of other men whom he did not recognise. Daniel later learned they were 'Pensioner Guards'. These men had all been career soldiers, having previously served around twenty years in the army. Some of them had been in the army since the young age of sixteen or seventeen, serving in far-off places such as India and the Crimea.

Their new employment as guards involved serving six months, plus twelve days a year after that. Their term had begun that day, tasked with guarding the prisoners for the duration of their transportation to Australia. In return for this service they were not only allowed to take with them their wives and children, but they would also be given a wage, a two-room cottage, and enough land for them to be able to grow some of their own food or to keep livestock.

Eventually Daniel and his fellow prisoners arrived down at the riverside. A place they knew well, having spent much of their time over the past few years labouring there.

Waiting for them were two steam-powered boats. The prisoners were then untethered from each other before being crammed onto the first boat, along with some of the warders. The remaining Pensioner Guards boarded the second boat.

The last guard had hardly had time to seat himself when the two boats moved off, taking a down-river to

Sheerness.

There were many sailing vessels of all different shapes and sizes tied up at Sheerness, including several British naval ships, which made a spectacular nautical scene fit for canvas.

As each ship came into view, Daniel wondered which would be the ship taking him to his new life. At first he assumed it was going to be one of the naval vessels, but as the boat he was on was clearly giving them a wide berth, he soon worked out this was not to be the case.

Towards the far end of the harbour, one of the vessels appeared to be moored slightly away from the others. On seeing it, Daniel had an inkling this could be the one they were heading for, and it wasn't long before the steamboat he was on began turning towards it.

They were a little over a ship's length from this vessel when Daniel spotted something between the forest of heads and bodies of his fellow prisoners. A nameplate on the stern of the ship. On first sight, he could only identify a few of the letters. The C, an R, and an A. There were other letters in between, but at this point they were still unclear. Gradually, as they drew closer, he was able to decipher more letters until everything became clear. It said 'Corona'.

The *Corona* was a brand-new steam- and sail-powered clipper ship. Designed internally for the transportation of convicts, she was on her first journey to the other side of the world. She was around two hundred feet long, thirty-five feet wide, had three large masts, and an iron hull. An unusual type of hull for a ship being used for such a journey.

This fact was soon spotted by one of the prisoners, who had a seafaring background. He started using his knowledge to try to calm some of the other prisoners near to him, assuring them that the iron hull was nothing to fear, and was perfectly able to float in all seas. Even though the prisoners had been forbidden to talk, the guards didn't attempt to stop him from giving the wisdom of his knowledge. Indeed some of the guards seemed to be glad to be hearing what he had to say too.

Standing on the deck, looking over the railings, was a group of women and children. It was obvious by their smiles, and the way they were waving towards the Pensioner Guards in the boat behind, that they were family members and would be travelling with them.

The convict beside Daniel muttered in a broad Irish accent, 'I never thought I'd get to see a nice woman again, let alone be on a boat with one.'

'That's why they've got you in chains!' replied Daniel, giving them both a chuckle.

They soon pulled up alongside a small jetty, and without delay were methodically removed from the boat and taken aboard the *Corona*.

Once on deck they were handed over to a deck guard, who removed their chains before whisking them down to the convict quarters below deck. At the far end was a row of metal doors, each leading to a small individual cell. The rest of the area was divided into a number of small, open sections. Big enough for about eight to a dozen men to sleep and eat in.

Daniel was taken past this open area and placed into one of the cells at the end. He wasn't sure if this was due to his continuing lack of remorse, and his desire to be transported to Australia, or simply that he was one of the first to be taken down.

The noise from all the cell doors being slammed behind the other convicts gave off a menacing, sinister sound. Daniel winced as the door slammed behind him. Without thought, he leaned his back against the cell wall and began slowly sliding down onto the floor. Something he had done many times before, in every cell he had previously been placed in. No sooner had he settled, he noticed that the noise from outside had become more muted, due to his own door having been closed, which came as a relief.

The process, as with everything else within the prison system, was well organised, so was all over in a short time.

Now and again, indecipherable voices emanated from the cells of the convicts, as they attempted to make contact with whoever was in the adjoining cell or in the area outside. These attempts were very soon quelled by the guards banging their truncheons on the cell doors, shouting at them to be silent, or making threats as to what would happen if they didn't obey.

Previously, when Daniel had been moved to a

new prison, he would be provided with food and drink fairly promptly, so he was hopeful things would be no different on board. But his hope was in vain, and it was several hours before the hatch finally opened, delivering the usual prisoner sustenance.

As he took his meal, he stooped down, peering out through the hatch and past the supplying hand in an attempt to get a glimpse of a face, willing it to be that of a fellow convict. Unfortunately it wasn't, but knowing he was unlikely to be sent back to land for talking, he decided to risk asking a question.

'When do we sail?'

'Quiet,' came the reply in an Irish accent. Daniel wondered if it was the convict who'd been next to him on the steamer, but it made no difference who it was, as the hatch was quickly bolted shut, stopping him from pressing for an answer.

Over the next few hours Daniel lost track of time. When another meal arrived, he guessed it was probably supper, so the likelihood of them sailing that day was rather unlikely.

After he had finished eating, he decided that he'd waited long enough for any orders or instructions to be given, and felt it was rather unlikely that any would now be forthcoming that day. So he opened up the hammock, which was rolled up in the corner of his cell, tied it up to the fixings, and no sooner had his head hit the canvas than he was drifting off to sleep.

He had barely dropped off when he was abruptly

woken by the cell door opening. In came a guard along with another man.

'Get up,' ordered the guard. As Daniel was obeying the instruction, the guard continued, 'This is the Reverend Williams, he's our religious instructor, who will be accompanying us on the voyage. He'll be taking a daily service, leading religious teachings, and be on hand to offer religious guidance. You can confide in him with all matters, should you wish, and he will have a few words with you now.'

With that, the guard stood outside, with the door partly open.

The Reverend Williams gave a nod of acknowledgement towards Daniel, and said, 'I am told your name is Phillips, and your crime was to have set fire to a stack?'

'Yes, sir,' replied Daniel, shuffling uneasily, with a feeling of embarrassment at having been reminded of his act by this stranger. Especially one who was standing in front of him with a Holy Bible tucked under his arm.

'So, Phillips, tell me, how you are feeling? I assume fairly anxious, wondering what the future may hold for you right now.'

'A little bit, but not that much,' replied Daniel in a nonchalant manner.

The Reverend Williams showed no reaction, having heard this 'manly' type of response several times already from other convicts. From past experience he knew that he would be unlikely to break through this hard exterior right now, so he continued his conversation with a different question.

'Would I be correct in saying that you've had a number of regrets of late, especially regarding your crime which has put you in this present situation?'

Daniel just shrugged his shoulders, remaining silent.

'Well, I will leave you for now, but maybe you will consider these things and decide whether you are fully repentant of your crime.'

Daniel wanted to say what was on his mind but was unsure whether this would be a prudent thing to do or not. But, taking a deep breath, he decided he might as well.

'I'm not sure that I am repentant, sir ... The stack was insured, and I neither caused or intended harm to any man. Maybe you think what I did was wrong, but I felt it was the only thing I could do. I couldn't see any other way of gaining a better life for myself, or to stop being a burden on my family.'

Daniel could see by the look in the Reverend's eyes that he wasn't at all taken aback by his lack of repentance, so he continued. 'My hope was, that once I've finished my sentence, I'll get to enjoy a new life in Australia. I must admit, I didn't understand how tough my sentence was going to be. But still, I have to say that, right now, I have no regrets at all.' Daniel paused again, realising that he was probably sounding far too arrogant, so he added, 'I can assure you, though, I have no desire to escape or cause trouble to any man here.'

The Reverend Williams still showed no sign of disapproval. Assuming Daniel had finished, he replied, 'I must say, Phillips, I acknowledge the honesty of your answer ... Anyway, think about what I've said, and if you wish, we could talk a little more about this, or anything else you wish, on another visit.'

Daniel mouthed 'Yeah,' as the Reverend continued.

'And one last thing, before I continue on my rounds. Are you at all nervous about the forthcoming journey across the waves?'

Daniel fleetingly raised his eyes in thought. 'Not really considered it, sir. I don't think so. You may not believe me from what I've said, but I have a faith in God, and have taken to prayer many a time in gaol. But I've not asked God to grant me safety on the voyage. Things have happened all too fast today to think about praying ... Maybe I should?'

The Reverend Williams gave an understanding look. 'In that case, will you join with me in a short prayer?'

'Yes, sir, I think that'll be of comfort to me,' replied Daniel as he put his hands together, bowed his head, and closed his eyes.

The Reverend Williams took this as his cue and said a prayer for the safety of the ship and all on board. As soon as he had finished with an 'Amen', he left the cell, turning his head towards Daniel as he went, saying, 'I look forward to having another meeting with you in a few days' time.'

'And I with you, Reverend,' responded Daniel. He said this not simply out of courtesy, but also with a genuine desire to have a conversation with him again.

As the guard was locking the door, Daniel called out to the Reverend.

'Sir, when do we sail?' However, no reply was forthcoming.

CHAPTER 13

On the Move

It was around four o'clock the following morning, and completely without warning, that Daniel was stirred from his sleep by a strange sensation coming from beneath him. It took a few seconds for him to properly awake, and for it to register that he wasn't having a dream, but the *Corona* was rocking gently from side to side.

Gradually Daniel could feel ever increasing movements, and with it, a smile began to spread across his face as he took in the fact they were at last on the move. To begin with, the movements gave off a calming, comforting feeling. However, it wasn't long before the *Corona* had developed a pronounced rolling motion, and it became obvious to all the convicts on board they were now heading out to sea.

Every now and then a loud cry of distress would bellow out from a frightened convict. One such cry was so clearly heard by Daniel that he was sure it came from someone in the cell directly next to his. Other than this, on the whole, everything was eerily silent as each convict was wrestling with his own thoughts and fears from what appeared to be the start of their journey. A journey from which they would probably never return. The crossing of the waves to the other side of the world.

After a quarter of an hour or so, the ship began leaning strongly to one side, as if it was turning. At the same time, she began rolling heavily up and down and side to side. Daniel tried to steady himself by holding on to the small table which was fixed to the side of his cell. As he was holding on, he could hear a growing number of cries coming from fellow convicts, all desperately wanting to escape from the ship, or at least escape the convict quarters and get on deck. One convict, who was clearly in the cell beside Daniel, had now become so violently sick that his vomiting made Daniel retch several times. So much that he needed to close his eyes and take several deep breaths with his hands over his ears to avoid being sick himself.

The petrified cries continued, until banging noises were heard from guards who had opened the hatch to the convict quarters, and who were now coming down the steps.

'Shut up! Be quiet!' came their shouts of displeasure.

At one point Daniel heard a guard shout that there was nothing wrong with the ship, they were only turning. This helped steady his own nerves, if not everyone else's.

Shortly after this, he heard another guard shouting something which puzzled him.

'It will be far worse than this when we get properly out to sea!'

Daniel couldn't understand why they were moving, if they weren't heading out to sea, bound for the Swan River Colony.

Daniel made his way over to the hatch, shouting for a guard. After only two or three calls the hatch opened, and he was firmly ordered to 'Shut up.' But before the guard could shut the hatch, Daniel had put his hand through the hole, stopping it from being closed.

'What's happening, where are we going?' he called out.

He expected to be told yet again to shut up, along with having his hand hit by either a truncheon or the hatch door. To his surprise, the guard looked through the hatch, saying, 'We'll be going up and down the coastline for a few weeks. One of the crew has been put ashore, suffering from cholera. The ship's gonna need a good clean – we need to be sure it's disease-free before taking on any more convicts.'

'More men?' questioned Daniel.

'Yeah, we're heading to Portsmouth, and then Portland.'

His apparent helpfulness then altered as he laughed, adding, 'After that you can say goodbye to Britain … For ever.'

Daniel swiftly withdrew his hand as the guard snapped the hatch closed.

Sitting down on the floor, Daniel began to dwell on

this interesting bit of information he'd just gained. As he was doing this, he became aware that the *Corona* had now settled down quite significantly. This fact had been missed by many of the other convicts, who had worked themselves up into such a state they were unaware things had eased. Various cries for help, along with the occasional noise of vomiting, could still be heard, and it took a while for the atmosphere below deck to completely settle down.

By the end of the next day, all on board seemed to have gained their sea legs. Although a few days later, while sailing off the South Downs, they encountered a severe storm. This caused such violent rolling of the ship that panic and sickness soon spread below deck once again, far surpassing that which they had experienced on their first day on the move.

During the storm, Daniel huddled himself up into a tight ball in the corner of his cell, using the two walls to stop himself being tossed from side to side. Even though this gave him little relief from the rising and falling motions of the ship, it was better than nothing, and he managed to ride out the storm.

CHAPTER 14

A Little Elaboration

The Reverend Williams visited Daniel at least once a week during the voyage. He would often stay for ten minutes or more, spending the time discussing many different subjects and issues with him.

He usually began by guiding their conversation on matters of faith, before following it up by enquiring on more personal things, such as how Daniel was coping with his confinement. Daniel always appreciated these visits, as it was one of the few occasions when he was at liberty to talk freely. He also got the impression that the Reverend was not only interested in talking about God, and Daniel's past sins, but was genuinely interested in him as a human being. Something which he hadn't experienced since the day of his conviction.

He was also well aware that the Reverend would be making notes, reporting back to the Surgeon Superintendent and the captain of the ship. He was also certain that once they had arrived at the convict establishment, a full report on him and his conduct would be given to the governor.

Because of this, Daniel took the first opportunity

that presented itself to yet again make it clear to the Reverend that he was not intending to cause any problems on board. He also made a point of mentioning something else, which had stemmed from a conversation he'd overheard as they were heading down-river to the *Corona*.

It had been relatively easy during this short trip for the men to snatch short conversations with each other. Overhearing one of these conversations, he had learned that some of the more trusted, less threatening convicts might be given a little more freedom on board, in order to help with the running of the ship. Having heard this story, Daniel figured it could be to his advantage if he was to mention some of the different types of work he had done in the past. Even if it meant stretching a point in the process.

It was during one of the Reverend's first visits to him that Daniel dropped into the conversation that he had previously helped out at his local village bakery. Although he did omit to tell him this was only for a week. Nevertheless, he thought it was worth saying anyway, in case help was ever required in the galley.

He also mentioned that he used to help the village doctor from time to time. As he was telling him this, he knew it was a silly thing to say as he was never likely to be of any use medically, or more to the point, if he really wanted it to be of use. This was mainly due to the fact that it was something of an elaboration of the truth. The reality of the situation was that Daniel's stepfather had been a friend of the village doctor. Then, one day, when Daniel was about fourteen, his mother and stepfather had to go away for a few days to attend a wedding. During their absence Daniel was sent to stay with the doctor, and during this stay he had first helped him. In as much as a fourteen-year-old could have done.

Although, being fairly literate, Daniel had been more of a help than a hindrance. So, over the next few years, he would occasionally be asked back to the doctor's home, usually on a Saturday, to help him out. Most of the time this simply involved tidying up or running errands. However, there were times when he would be asked to do other things, such as mixing up, or the dispensing of medicines. In return the doctor would give him a couple of pennies, and his wife would usually provide a little lunch. This tended to be a nice thick soup or stew in the winter, with fresh bread. In the summer, it tended to be either cheese or cold meats. He was always very glad if he arrived and could smell the aroma of a nice fruit cake baking, as he always got to enjoy a slice as well as the fragrance.

CHAPTER 15

Having Faith

During Daniel's time as a convict, many dates became forever etched in his memory. Two of which were the fifteenth and sixteenth of October.

On the fifteenth, all convicts on board the *Corona* were given pen and paper, and were permitted to write one last letter home to a loved one, before finally leaving the shores of Britain. Daniel wrote a letter to his mother. He informed her of his pending departure and begged her for forgiveness. He also told her that he would write again, once he reached the convict establishment, and asked her to send a reply. He wasn't sure if she would do this, or even if she did, whether it would ever be delivered to him. Still, he knew he needed to cling on to what little hope he could, even if it was no more than a glimmer of hope.

On the sixteenth, the Reverend Williams visited Daniel again, this time bringing two pieces of especially welcome news.

'I've come to let you know, we are leaving these shores today.' He had begun speaking even before he had fully entered Daniel's cell, and he was clearly in a hurry. 'We will be finally weighing anchor later this afternoon. Full steam and sail ahead for Australia.'

Surprisingly to the Reverend, Daniel didn't say anything. He just stood there, with an almost vacant look. Everything was now feeling a little too surreal, and he wasn't sure how to respond. For at last he was about to begin that long-awaited journey across the seas. Heading towards the land of his dreams, on the other side of the globe. Yet he did not know what to say, how to react, or even how he was feeling inside.

The Reverend Williams continued with his second piece of news. 'I have been asked to appoint some convicts to assist with the daily running of the ship. Men who have developed a more trustworthy nature since their convictions. I believe you to be of such character. So tomorrow, once we are out on the open seas, you'll be released from your cell and be given the position of the captain of a mess. You will be in charge of seven other convicts.'

Daniel's face lit up. Finding his tongue, he said, 'Thank you, thank you so much for recommending me for this position, sir.' He then gave a smug smile, satisfied that his various exaggerated tales of previous jobs seemed to have paid off.

'One other thing ... don't let me down, or yourself for that matter,' warned the Reverend, with a stern tone.

'No, I won't do that, sir. I promise I'll make every effort to prove your trust in me was well placed,' replied Daniel.

The Reverend Williams did not engage in any further conversation, leaving as speedily as he'd entered.

Daniel remained standing in the same spot for several minutes, his head spinning with all sorts of emotions, both good and bad. He was happy to be finally leaving England's shores, and that his plan was continuing. But all his thoughts of this were tainted by the knowledge that he was unlikely ever to return to Britain, or see his family ever again.

Just as he was beginning to feel a little emotional at this, his mood was lifted by pleasant thoughts, that he'd no longer need to endure a life of working outside in either the damp or freezing cold British weather. As he was dwelling on this, something else crossed his mind which hadn't occurred to him up till then. If the weather was too hot in Australia, would he be able to cope with working in it? This thought bothered him, but only for a moment as his thoughts now turned towards food.

The prison food which had been dished out over the past few years had been of a very basic, tasteless nature. In fact it had been far worse than he had ever imagined it was going to be. Furthermore, he had little hope, if any, of there being an improvement at the next establishment. He had heard rumours that it would be a little better, but he wasn't optimistic about this. Even so, he comforted himself with the thought that at least he would still be getting regular meals while serving the remainder of his sentence.

Finally, as he was pondering these things, his

thoughts turned towards the impending journey, and facing life in a new gaol. Was the ship clear of the cholera outbreak, and would he, and the ship, survive the journey? Coming from the heart of the countryside, he had always assumed that ships were mostly made of wood. Having spent the past few weeks on board the *Corona*, with its iron hull, he knew this wasn't the case, and was doubting her ability to float on the open sea. This was despite all the reassurances he'd previously heard, and having witnessed how well the ship had coped with the storms which it had already been buffeted by.

Daniel was also troubled by thoughts of his looming life inside Fremantle Gaol. He had already heard some very worrying tales about the harshness of the regime out there. Some of which sent shivers down his spine. Although he did have it on good authority, from Reverend Williams, that there would be no forced use of the crank or treadwheel there. This was tremendously good news, and a comforting thought in the midst of the other concerning matters.

***

It was around three thirty in the afternoon when the *Corona* finally weighed anchor from off the coastline of Portland. Once again she began slowly rocking from side to side, and with ever increasing movements began heading out to sea. There were one or two cries of distress to be heard, but the vast majority of convicts were now resigned to the fact that nothing would stop them from being transported to the other side of the world. Sailing up and down the coastline for a number of weeks, and being hit by one or two storms in the process, had also helped prepare them for the long journey ahead.

CHAPTER 16

Australia-Bound

The following morning, Daniel awoke to begin his first day at sea without any land in sight. Shortly after breakfast a guard came, issuing him with a sheet of paper, full of instructions on how to go about his duty as captain of a mess. At first he was delighted at being given this position, but having read all his instructions and responsibilities, he was far less keen on the idea.

Among the many duties on his list, one was to assign each of the men in his mess certain tasks each day. These included such things as washing up after meals, washing their clothes and bedding, and making sure the men were keeping themselves bodily clean. On top of that, he had to keep a constant, watchful eye on the men. Making sure they behaved according to the rules, and that nothing ever went missing. If he failed, he would be held partly responsible, possibly suffering a share of the punishment that was handed out to the offenders.

Another important task, which needed to be meticulously carried out, was scrubbing the decks and whitewashing all the cells with chloride of lime. This was needed to help keep infectious diseases under control. Especially in light of the sailor who was found to have been suffering from cholera when the *Corona* had arrived at Sheerness.

There had also been two other men on board, convicts William Sharpe and Enoch Gibson, who had died the previous month from sickness and disease while anchored off Portland and Portsmouth.

Daniel was a mild tempered, meek natured man, so the thought of having to give orders to some of the rough, sharp-tongued criminals who were on board filled him with much anxiety and trepidation.

Having finished reading the list of instructions, he decided that under the circumstances, the most sensible thing to do would be to assign himself to some of the less desirable tasks, rather than saving all the slightly easier ones for himself. He hoped this would not only show the other men that he was mucking in with them, but it would also help him to keep an eye on them too.

However, the first duty of the day was to collect the midday meal, portioning it out to the rest of the men in his mess. This gave Daniel an idea, which meant he certainly wasn't going to be passing this duty on to another man, at least not for a few days.

Thankfully, some of the rules on the convict ship were a little more relaxed than he had encountered in the various prisons on land. On board, convicts were permitted to talk with each other freely, as long as they were not too loud, disruptive, and did not swear.

Conversing with the guards or members of the crew, on the other hand, was still strictly prohibited, unless they had good reason for doing so. Nevertheless, when Daniel first went to collect the food, he leaned towards the cook and thanked him, trusting that would probably be acceptable. But then in a low voice added a complimentary remark about the look of the food.

The following morning, on his way to collect breakfast, he found the guard standing outside the galley. So having seemingly got away with his remarks the day before, he grasped the opportunity before him and made some further comments to the cook.

'That dinner ya cooked yesterday, it was delightful.'

'You being sarcastic?' replied the cook, with a glare.

'No, indeed not, sir. I meant it. It was tasty, just the right amount of salt in it. The grub in Chatham was nothin' to be desired, but your cooking reminded me of what my mother gave us.' He then purposely added, 'Sometimes I would help her in the kitchen too.'

The cook just eyed Daniel up and down, handed him some loaves of bread, and motioned with the back of his hand for him to leave.

Daniel was unsure how this fraternisation had been taken by the cook, and if he would now be reported for trying to engage in conversation. Still, he thought it worth the risk for several reasons. One of these being that two of the men under him were especially unsavoury characters. He was already fearing the worst if he was to remain in charge of them, so if his approach to the cook resulted in the loss of his position, it would at least be one less thing to worry about. Daniel was certainly not out to deliberately lose his position, as it had given him the chance to have contact with the cook, which was an important part of his scheme. He also figured, or at least hoped, that if he was able to get on the cook's good side, then at some point during the voyage it may lead to a position assisting him.

The general daily life on board was not too dissimilar to that of prison life on land. Strict, structured, done to the clock – or at least the ship's bell.

The day began at 4.30 a.m. Then at 6 a.m. the heads of each mess would need to fill the washtubs on deck, before making sure all men under their charge were properly cleansed. Breakfast would be served in their individual mess groups at 8 a.m., with prayers following at 9.30 a.m. These were said by the religious instructor, up on deck, sea conditions permitting.

Following prayers, the convicts were divided off into two sections. One half would remain on deck for exercise before carrying out tasks such as scrubbing the decks or jobs below deck, which sometimes included making prisoners' clothing. They usually made a good job of this, in case they ended up wearing them at some point in the future.

Meanwhile, the other section of men would be arranged in schools, which were under the supervision of the religious instructor. In the afternoon the two groups would swap over. Supper was at 4.30 p.m., and more prayers were held at 6 p.m. Finally, all the men had to be in their hammocks by 8.30 p.m.

One big difference to that of prison life on land was that now everything depended on the weather and sea conditions. During the voyage they encountered more than their fair share of storms and squalls, and many a day saw disruptions to their itinerary. The first of these began in the late afternoon and continued long into the evening on their first full day at sea.

Until then most of the convicts, including Daniel, thought they'd become accustomed to any rough sea conditions that might come their way. But they quickly discovered, with the storm which hit them on that first day, that they hadn't yet gained their sea legs. Indeed, almost all on board were sick, which included some of the seasoned crew too.

During the storm the convicts were locked securely into the convict area below deck. On top of everything else, this gave rise to a general feeling of claustrophobia, and no sooner had one of the men begun vomiting, than it set off a chain reaction among many of the other convicts.

Half an hour into the storm, six guards came down the steps to the convict quarters, bringing with them three barrels and two sacks. Most of the convicts were too ill to notice the guards, but Daniel, who was suffering a little less than many, had spotted them and made eye contact with the leading guard. He approached Daniel first, handing him a small mug from the bag he was carrying. He told him to hold it under the brass tap that was sticking out from the barrel which another guard was holding. This was no easy task to perform, with the ship rolling up and down so heavily, but by sitting upright on his knees and keeping his back to the side of the ship, he just about managed it.

Once his mug was in place, the guard opened the barrel tap, allowing the liquid to half fill the mug. Then, in one motion he closed the tap and moved on to the next man, who he hoped was capable of doing the same without too much bother.

Daniel peered into the mug with suspicion, wondering what the liquid was. Lime juice was regularly given out, as a cure for scurvy, but this time Daniel thought it may have been wine. He wasn't too sure, as it was far too dark below deck to see clearly, and he'd only had the pleasure of drinking such a luxury on a few special occasions before. Furthermore, being on a prison ship in the middle of a storm didn't seem like something to celebrate. Unless the guards were more sadistic than he thought, which at this point he still hadn't ruled out.

As he was looking into his mug, the ship rolled sharply to the side, causing some of the liquid to slop onto the back of his hand. Daniel put his hand up to his nose, attempting to smell it but without success, as the smell of his own vomit and that of others around him was masking all other smells. He licked the back of his hand. It was wine. Daniel laughed out loud and, turning towards the other convicts in his mess area, some of whom were already drinking, raised the mug above his head and shouted, 'Good health, everyone.'

He later discovered this was a very apt thing to have said, as the Surgeon Superintendent was under the belief that, medically speaking, a little wine helped the stomach cope much better with both stress and seasickness. Daniel was unconvinced by this theory, but wine was dished out several times during the voyage, particularly when encountering rough storms, and he wasn't going to be the one to question this wisdom.

CHAPTER 17

New Life

Daniel had been captain of a mess for less than two weeks when something occurred that went on to have great implications involving an incident that was to take place many years later.

It was shortly after the wake-up call on the morning of the twenty-fifth of October, while getting the washtub ready on deck, that he was approached by one of the guards.

'Phillips, you are no longer to be a mess captain.'

Simultaneously those words filled Daniel with two very contrasting thoughts. On the one hand, relief that he was no longer in danger of suffering from someone else's misdemeanour. On the other, he was worried that his constant attempts to gain favour with the cook were about to land him in severe trouble.

The guard continued, 'You are to report at once to Dr Crawford, the Surgeon Superintendent. He needs help for a few days. We have several sick on board, and apparently you've helped a doctor before.'

Daniel started to panic, assuming his over-elaborations to the Reverend Williams were now about to get him into a spot of bother. However, before he had time to think how to explain away the reality of the matter, the guard had ordered him to go, and Daniel found himself heading towards the surgeon's quarters at haste.

On arrival, and after the briefest of introductions, he was ordered to take a pile of bloodied towels and soiled sheets to be washed, then to locate and bring back some clean ones. How these towels had become so bloodstained he didn't know, nor did he wish to find out. As for the soiled sheets, this took very little working out and gave him great cause for concern. He knew this couldn't be down to rough seas as they had been pleasantly calm the previous few days. However, it was now common knowledge that a number of men on board had been suffering from choleretic diarrhoea. Indeed, Enoch Gibson had died from this, so Daniel was more than a little worried that all the laundry he was now carrying may have been a result of another cholera case. At that moment he would have given anything to have still been the captain of a mess.

After he'd finished boiling the laundry, he hung it out on a wooden rack to dry. The rigging would have made a far better line, but that was strictly prohibited.

Having then gathered some new sheets and towels, he returned to the surgeon's quarters. As he was raising his hand to knock on the cabin door, he heard a short, sharp, and fairly loud cry from inside, clearly coming from someone who was in pain. Daniel paused for a moment, unsure whether to enter. The cry sounded again. It was a rather high-pitched cry, as if being let out by a woman.

Knowing he couldn't wait outside all day, and would have to enter at some point, he knocked hard on the door and stepped inside. Before he was able to close the door behind him, he was struck motionless to the spot by the scene before him. Only a few feet away, with his back towards him, was a Pensioner Guard, looking down towards a patient on a bed. Dr Crawford was standing on the other side of the bed, attending to a very distressed woman, a heavily pregnant woman at that.

Dr Crawford looked up at Daniel. 'Quick, man, run – bring me a pail of boiling water, and some more clean towels.'

Without any hesitation Daniel put the clean linen he'd been carrying on a small table and rushed off to gather the required things.

Approaching the cabin on his return, he saw two guards standing outside, talking to each other. He could see by the stature of one of them that he was the guard who had been inside the cabin with the patient. Daniel hadn't seen his face earlier, but he now recognised him as Captain Hughes, the Pensioner Guard that had brought in the wine during the first storm out at sea.

Passing the two guards, Daniel began feeling extremely uncomfortable with the whole situation so avoided looking at them as he went inside.

Almost as soon as he had closed the door, the patient hollered again with what seemed to be an even sharper, more piercing cry than before. Daniel stood, staring at the woman on the bed, unconsciously swinging the pail of boiled water in one hand, while squeezing the towels very tightly with his other arm.

The patient was lying on the bed, with her bare legs and knees in the air, and her night gown covering very little past her waist. Daniel had never seen so much of a woman's leg before. As a result, he could feel his face becoming uncomfortably warm, and was aware that his cheeks were now taking on a glaringly obvious red glow. To make matters worse, and despite the fact he was in the cabin under orders, he still felt incredibly guilty at being in the middle of this private, and exceedingly intimate, situation. One which even her own husband wasn't permitted to be witness to.

Dr Crawford had been holding a damp cloth on the woman's forehead when Daniel entered but, noticing he had failed to move beyond the closed door, he straightened the cloth on the lady's forehead before calmly going over to Daniel. Taking the pail of boiled water from his hand, he said with a low whisper, 'This is most irregular having you here at this time. Unfortunately, I fear this could be a difficult birth, so I may well be in need of a little help. Having been informed of your previous, albeit limited experience of working with a doctor, and given this situation, I think it's best you stay here.'

'Erm, well, I've not actually had any experience with giving birth, sir ... Well, only with sheep!' replied Daniel. He hadn't intended the comment to come across in such a flippant manner, but as soon as the words had left his mouth he knew that it had come over that way.

Fortunately, Dr Crawford gave a slight grin, saying, 'Well, it's probably not that different. Just don't let Mrs Hughes know.' Then pointing to the far side of the cabin, and still whispering, said, 'Over there is one of my aprons in that trunk. Put it on, and do everything I say. But don't look embarrassed at what you are seeing – you must appear to be professional. If necessary, pretend she is one of your sheep!'

Daniel smiled at this, not only finding it amusing that a doctor should speak with such humour, but also with relief that his own previous comment had not angered him. It also left him feeling a lot more relaxed about the situation, and he felt his face instantly cooling down.

For the next half hour Daniel did little other than stand beside Mrs Hughes, holding a damp flannel over her forehead. He also spent a great deal of that time simply staring around the room, preferring to study any object he could see, other than having to focus on what was unfolding on the bed before him.

At one point, as he was watching a fly crawling across the far wall of the cabin, his gaze was abruptly diverted back towards the bed. Both Mrs Hughes and Dr Crawford's movements had now become noticeably more exaggerated, accompanied by an ever increasing amount of noise from Mrs Hughes. Suddenly, and without any warning, a small baby's head began to appear just below her rolled-up gown, and into the hands of Dr Crawford. The head was rapidly followed by the rest of its body, and at that very moment the cries of pain from Mrs Hughes ceased, and seemingly without a pause were followed by the sound of crying from this precious new life before them.

Without being asked, Daniel grabbed one of the clean towels which he had brought back earlier and handed it to the doctor, who then wrapped it around the baby before handing the newborn to Mrs Hughes. 'You appear to have a healthy baby boy,' he declared.

Dr Crawford moved around the bed, and coming close to Daniel, discreetly thanked him for his assistance before telling him to go back to the convict quarters and wait until he was called for again. As Daniel turned to leave, Dr Crawford added, 'On your way, please inform Mr Hughes of the safe arrival of his son, and that he can now enter to see his wife and child.'

Daniel did this with a feeling of pride and importance. Not only from having been entrusted to take part in such an amazing event, but also that he'd been asked to deliver the good news to the baby's father.

Daniel came into contact with Mr Hughes many more times during the voyage, but each time the encounter felt more than a little awkward. These were occasions when both men behaved as if nothing had ever happened that day, and not a word was ever spoken between them again regarding the birth. Although, a week later, the Reverend Williams informed Daniel that he'd carried out a christening for the baby, who had been named Thomas. He also mentioned that Mrs Hughes had asked for her, and her husband's, gratefulness be conveyed to Daniel for his help in the safe arrival of their son. Which was a surprise to him as he felt he'd done very little that day, other than to hold a damp cloth and fetch things. Still, he was glad of the appreciation, as any good mark towards his character report could only be of benefit to him.

CHAPTER 18

Never a Dull Moment

Daniel assisted Dr Crawford for the next three days in a row, and on a few other occasions too. He was thankful that at no time did he witness anything as dramatic as had happened on his first day. Indeed most of the time he was either cleaning or running messages for him. These were mainly to patients, enquiring on their progress, or delivering messages to the ship's captain, William Croudace.

Fortunately for Daniel, he never regained his position as captain of a mess, and things were soon to turn out infinitely better for him.

To his surprise, the attempts to fraternise with the ship's cook had actually paid off, and after spending a short period of time assisting Dr Crawford, he was sent to assist the cook, along with two other convicts.

Although his cooking skills were almost non-existent, his duties were usually nothing more than preparing vegetables, cutting up meat, baking bread, or handing out the food to the mess captains. There were times when his inexperience was evident, but with quick thinking he was always able to bluff his way around the situation. In any case, things were rarely a problem, as everything was carried out under the close supervision of the ship's cook, who was not only very experienced, but was also a tolerant man, so everything usually ran happily and smoothly.

Occasionally, he would be tasked with the preparation and serving of meals for the guards and crew. This he relished, as it gave him the chance to secretly sample a better selection of food than was dished out to the convicts.

The position as a cook's assistant not only gave Daniel more freedom, but it also gave him opportunities to engage in lengthy conversations with his co-workers. Especially with his fellow convict assistants, Edward McDougall and William Harper.

To Daniel's astonishment, they had both been convicted for the same reason he had: the arson of stacks. Edward claimed it had happened when he accidentally dropped a match while having a smoke by a stack. William said he had done it for exactly the same reason as Daniel: the chance of having a new life in the warmer climes of Australia.

Being present at the birth of Captain Hughes' son was by far the most dramatic event Daniel encountered on the *Corona*, but the rest of the voyage was certainly not without any incident or interest.

On one occasion, while working in the galley, sounds of great laughter and frivolity were heard coming from the upper deck. On hearing this, the cook went over to the guard, and having gained his permission, they were all permitted to investigate the cause of the commotion. They witnessed the hilarious spectacle of a ship's officer dancing around the deck in front of a large number of Pensioner Guards and crew, all of whom were offering a great deal of raucous encouragement.

The officer was wrapped in a toga made from an old sheet. He was also wearing a crown, had a long false beard, and was carrying a three-pronged pitchfork. Then, as his energy and enthusiasm seemed to be waning, he was handed a large pail of water, and he proceeded to completely drench one of the crew members who had been standing slightly removed from the rest of the onlookers. The man cowered slightly as the pail was raised, yet he seemed to be more than a little prepared for what was about to happen, and he put up no resistance. This soaking was then followed up by several other buckets of water being flung from other crew members.

The cook could see that Daniel appeared somewhat bemused by this whole performance and hadn't a clue what was going on. So the cook explained to Daniel that he'd been witnessing an old sailing tradition. Neptune, the officer, had 'baptised' one of the crew members, who had just crossed over the equator for the first time.

On another occasion, while returning from delivering dinner to Captain Croudace, he witnessed a fellow convict, Thomas Hinson, being buried at sea by his mess mates, with the Reverend Williams in attendance, conducting a very short service. Daniel had met Thomas only two days previously, while spending the afternoon working for Dr Crawford. He had explained to Daniel that the patient was extremely sick, which was obvious, but Daniel hadn't taken Dr Crawford's explanation as an indication of the man's imminent demise.

Another major incident took place one morning, in late November, which made Daniel appreciate how immensely fortunate he had been with events conspiring in his favour.

They had been at sea about six weeks, sailing off the southern coast of Africa, when Daniel heard loud shouting and men running around the decks. At the time he was working in the galley and, wondering what was happening, he stopped what he was doing and was thinking about going to investigate when a guard came rushing in and began aggressively pushing Daniel, Edward, and William towards the door, ordering them to return post-haste to the convict section below deck.

As they hastily made their way back, wondering what was going on, they encountered lots of other guards, who were also rushing around with the same urgency, also ordering any convicts they could find to return to the convict quarters.

It soon transpired that the ship's carpenter had discovered a number of small holes had been bored through a section of planks between decks, in the form of a square. It was clear that this had been intended for completion at a later date, and to be used as an escape hatch, for it was just about big enough for a man to squeeze through.

Without delay, the upper surface of the deck in the convict area was thoroughly searched. To begin with, no trace of any cuts to the planks could be found, as they had been so cleverly disguised with paper and soap. Indeed, they were only found later by pushing a piece of wire from below, which helped locate the cuts under the boards of the bed of a convict.

Two men, George Egan and John Barker, whose beds were above the place, were selected for corporal punishment, and at noon each man received twenty-four lashes. The captain of their mess, Hugh McGriskin, received eighteen lashes as his share, for failing to keep control of the men under his supervision.

This came as an enormous shock to Daniel, as these were the men who had originally been in his mess. Had he not been sent to work for the surgeon, and then the cook, with the addition of being placed in a different mess group, he would now have been suffering the very punishment which had been carried out on Hugh McGriskin.

McGriskin and Egan were the two men that Daniel had feared were the most likely to cause trouble. Both had come across as rather unsavoury characters from the start. Daniel had been concerned that Egan, who had been convicted for burglary and wounding, may have been more than a little tempted to steal things if given the chance. As for McGriskin, Daniel wasn't at all surprised to learn he'd been made captain of the mess, as he'd been convicted of manslaughter, and few in his mess were likely to resist his orders. It was for this reason Daniel strongly suspected he had been well aware of, and more than likely heavily involved in, the creation of the escape plan.

There were two other memorable incidents which occurred during the voyage that stuck in Daniel's mind. Both of these involved something going overboard.

One day, Samuel Georgetti, who was originally from Italy and had already showed a rather fiery nature, became excessively frustrated with what he considered to be badly fitting clothes. The guard's refusal to issue more suitable ones didn't help the situation, so he threw all of his clothes overboard! He was then given a new set of clothing, but along with them he was also given a length of time in solitary confinement.

The other incident took place one Sunday morning, during a divine service which was being held on deck for the Roman Catholics. As the service was drawing to a close, one of the crew members, who was watching from the side, fell overboard. Double quick, a lifebuoy was thrown out to him, and the ship's lifeboat was hastily lowered into the sea. Fortunately, within a few minutes he was successfully rescued and brought back on board to dry out.

Compared to the time Daniel had already spent in gaol, and what was to come at Fremantle, he considered his time on the *Corona* a rather enjoyable one. Even with the rules, regulations, and added storms thrown in.

Daniel often thought that he would have been more than happy spending the entirety of his sentence at sea. Of course, this was never going to be an option, but if it could have been, he would have taken it.

After they had crossed the equator, heading ever closer towards their destination, they left most of the storms behind, leaving them to enjoy many continuous days of calm blue seas and cloudless sunny skies. The ship's steady movement created a pleasant, cooling breeze, and in spending a lot of his time up and around the deck in the sunshine, Daniel had acquired a rather healthy tan by the time his voyage had come to an end.

During the latter part of the voyage, Daniel had the pleasure of witnessing the wonderful sight of a pod of bottlenose dolphins coming very close to the ship. A sight he never forgot. Another time he spotted some flying fish, and once, although it was a little way off in the distance, he caught sight of the spurting spout and tail of a large whale. All were such amazing sights, ones that he would never have had the privilege of witnessing had he not taken the course he had chosen.

The incredibly well-designed *Corona*, with its steam and sail, coped more than adequately with the many storms, squalls, and choppy sea conditions they encountered en route. As a result of this, they made such a speedy voyage that when they arrived off the coast of Fremantle, the crossing had only taken sixty-seven days. This was the fastest crossing of a convict ship which had ever been made.

CHAPTER 19

Land Ahoy

'Land ahoy,' came the cry from one of the guards, who had popped his head into the galley before disappearing just as quick. Daniel, William Harper, and the head cook were the only ones working in the galley at the time. The cook seemed unmoved by the news, but Daniel and William had a real longing to go on deck to see land again.

Daniel had been chopping vegetables and pushed some of the remaining ones towards William for him to finish off. Then, sidling up to the head cook, Daniel asked if he could clean the large cooking pots which had been used for breakfast.

The cook chuckled, knowing the real reason why he wanted to do this, but seemed at ease in giving Daniel, and William, permission to do so.

Daniel and William picked up as many pots and pans as they could carry and took them on deck to a washing tub. They dumped them into the water without care and made their way over to the far side of the ship, in the hope of getting their first sight of Australia and the land of their dreams.

Land was still a long way off, yet visible. Daniel and William stood still, neither saying a word to each other, even though they were thinking the same thing.

William broke the silence. 'It ain't very big, is it?'

'I don't believe it. I've gone through all this, only to end up on that tiny little island. I thought Australia was massive,' Daniel said, utterly dejected.

One of the crew was nearby, so they took a chance and spoke to him.

'Australia's smaller than we thought.'

The man roared with laughter. 'You fools, that's Rottnest Island. It's about ten miles from Australia.'

Daniel and William looked at each other with relief and began laughing hysterically at themselves.

As the mainland was still not in sight, they didn't bother hanging about on deck, but returned to the tub of pots and pans. They had just rolled up their sleeves when a guard approached, ordering them to go back to the convict quarters at once.

Climbing down the hatch, they discovered the rest of their fellow convicts had already been assembled there. Speculation was rife as to what was about to happen, but they didn't have long to find out, as a group of guards soon came down, each carrying a large canvas bag.

'We've got some early Christmas gifts for you,' shouted out one of the guards, laughing.

'You will love these gifts,' added the guard behind him. With that he reached into the bag, producing a shackle. He held it up for all to see, and a deathly silence fell throughout the convict quarters.

Having spent most of the past two months unshackled, and free, to now being placed back into restraints came as a sharp wake-up call to Daniel. The discomfort of the irons, along with the knowledge that he was soon to be locked up behind a prison wall once again, played greatly on his mind for several hours. As it did with the other convicts locked below deck with him.

Shortly after noon a ship's pilot, Mr Jackson, came alongside in a small boat and boarded the *Corona*, although Daniel was unaware of this.

Two hours later the *Corona* weighed anchor, with Mr Jackson bringing her towards port. They finally cast anchor at three o'clock, just off Fremantle, on the mouth of the Swan River.

The convicts, still locked below deck, were unable to see what was going on or where they were, yet all knew the sea voyage had almost come to an end, and they became increasingly fidgety and vocal.

The unpleasantness of having spent the past few hours in chains, concern about what was to come, and the anticipation of reaching land once again, was becoming all too much to cope with for Daniel and his fellow convicts.

Another two long hours passed by, still without any sign of movement, or information forthcoming as to what was going to happen next. The inactivity and boredom now caused many of the men, including

Daniel, to begin dozing off to sleep.

Sometime later, a sudden noise from the hatch being opened stirred those who were asleep. The guards who had earlier delivered the chains reappeared. This time bringing with them supper, along with news that they were going to be spending one last night on board the *Corona*.

This news was met with a mixed and considerably noisy response. For once the guards didn't even attempt to silence them. The noise quietened a little as they passed the food around, then rose again as they left, locking the hatch behind them. It seemed the guards had probably expected the noisy reaction, as they made no fuss, and no sooner had the hatch closed than the noise from the convicts abated.

After they had finished eating, most of the men retired to their hammocks, although a few remained lying on the floor all night. Each and every one lost in their own individual thoughts. Thoughts of their past crimes, far away families, and wondering what the forthcoming regime was about to inflict upon them. All of these things ensured that none of them enjoyed the benefit of a good night's sleep. Something they could have done with to help them face the following day's uncertainties.

In the morning, breakfast had barely been consumed when the Comptroller General and the commandant from the convict establishment boarded the *Corona*. They had arrived to thoroughly inspect the ship, giving special attention to the convicts, and making sure that no disease was rife on board. Once they had been satisfied, they returned to the prison, but not before leaving behind a piece of unwelcome news ... The *Corona* would not be permitted to unload its cargo of convicts until the following morning. So, Daniel and his fellow convicts had to spend yet another day and night locked up in the convict area below deck.

The rest of that day dragged by frustratingly for the men, and they had nothing more to occupy their time with, other than to dwell even more on their pasts and futures. Some also tried to work out a way of escape, and openly discussed their new plans with those around them. One or two were ridiculously fanciful ideas, indeed even the ones who were creating the plans knew it, but it gave them hope, and helped pass the time.

Egan and Barker, two of the men who had earlier been involved in the plan to create an escape hatch, were sitting not too far from Daniel, looking rather dejected. On hearing the plans around them, they began to feel that their plan was actually quite a good one and made this known to those sitting nearby. The other convicts agreed, but this seemed to make Egan and Barker even more downcast. Daniel also quite admired their plan, and even though he had no desire himself to escape, he felt pity for them. He called over to them, trying to make them feel a little better about the situation. 'You'd never have made it far though. Not in those chains.' The two men looked at each other, suddenly realising that this problem hadn't once crossed their minds. Not in the initial planning, or even now, as they had been sitting there. Daniel's comment took a few seconds to sink in, but when it did, both men began to see a little of the funny side of it. Despite having gone through a flogging for nothing.

For all the convicts, their minds had become so dulled and exhausted with the boredom of being locked below, that by the evening most of them dropped off to sleep and managed to get a relatively good night's rest.

CHAPTER 20

Fremantle Convict Establishment

Sunday, 24 December 1866

At the crack of dawn, and without having any breakfast, the convicts were assembled in their mess groups and gradually led up onto the main deck.

Before any man could get even the slightest idea about going over the rails and making a swim for it, they were chained together in small groups. This was carried out in the same way as it had been three months earlier, when leaving Chatham.

As Daniel was standing on the deck, with the early morning Australian sun beaming down from an almost cloudless sky, he remembered that it was Christmas Eve.

Thoughts flooded back of those awful wintery days through which he'd once lived and worked, back in Great Hadham. He could still vividly remember all the dark, gloomy wet days, when he would have to work from dawn to dusk on the farm.

Just as clear in his memory were the bitter cold

winds and frosty, snowy, icy weather conditions, which had never seemed to completely go before another such spell followed on. Going hand in hand with this would be night times of very little sleep due to the cold.

Daniel raised his head towards the sky. The glorious Western Australian sun was warming his face, wrapping itself around his whole body. The feeling was far better than he had even imagined.

Perhaps I should have fired a stack many years ago, he thought to himself.

He closed his eyes, lapping up the sunshine as if he had not a care in the world. As he stood with his eyes still closed, he felt someone being chained next to him, then heard footsteps, presumably those of a guard, moving away.

Daniel opened one eye to see an older, sullen-faced convict beside him. He had been part of another mess, and until now their paths on board ship had never met sufficiently long enough, or close enough, to have engaged in any meaningful conversation. He decided to offer up a pleasantry. 'Isn't it a lovely day? Think I'm gonna like it here!'

The convict huffed, 'Ya won't be smiling soon, son. They ain't letting you go free, ya know. You're being locked up again, and it will be for many more years.'

'I don't care. That ain't ever stopped me smiling,' replied Daniel, with a dogged determination.

As the last word left his mouth, a loud voice bellowed out from beside him, 'No talking.'

This command was immediately followed up by the crunching thump of a guard's forearm striking across the back of his shoulder. Daniel stumbled forward, but due to the constraints of the chains he fell onto the convict in front of him, sending them both down to their knees in a tangled heap.

The guard hauled Daniel back up. 'Talk again, and you'll be going straight to the punishment cell when we get there,' he said, glaring at Daniel before walking off.

Out of earshot, Daniel quickly regained his humour. From the corner of his mouth he whispered to the convict he'd just fallen on, 'Another prison in another land, yet still the same lovely welcome!'

It seemed to take considerably longer to remove the convicts from the *Corona* than it had taken to get them on board two months earlier. This didn't bother them though, as each man knew a cell would soon be awaiting their arrival, and standing outside in the glorious sunshine seemed a far better option.

Once all of the convicts had been chained up, they gradually disembarked, and were made to stand in a line along the jetty. Here the guards began counting them, making certain that nobody had hidden away unnoticed.

A brief check was then made to ensure that all of the chains had been securely locked in place. Once satisfied, the guards took their places in front, behind, and at either side of the long column of convicts.

The families of the Pensioner Guards had left the ship an hour beforehand, along with their luggage, and had been escorted away in horse-drawn carriages to begin life in their newly built homes.

The procession of convicts now began its clinking shuffle away from the harbour. Daniel took one last look back towards the *Corona* with a feeling of sadness inside. With his hands shackled in front of him, he gave a small, symbolic wave, to say goodbye.

Those past few weeks aboard her had, in a strange sort of way, been a very peaceful period in his life. He turned his head away, wondering if he'd made the wrong decision on that snowy January morning, and whether he should have tried to join the Navy instead. He didn't dwell on this for long though, as he knew such thoughts would easily bring him down, so as quickly as the thought had surfaced, he banished it from his mind.

The column made its way slowly along a well-built road, on the outskirts of Fremantle. From what Daniel could see, it appeared to be a nicely developing town. A rather pleasant-looking place. He felt it was the sort of town that he might like to settle down in one day, and be likely to find work in. At the same time, Daniel knew he was really a country boy at heart, so something on a farm would probably be better suited to him. Either way, he knew he had a sentence to complete first, before having to make any such decision on where to live or work.

It wasn't a great distance from the harbour to the prison, but the walk was a far from easy task. Trying to put one foot in front of the other while being chained to a group of other men, who in turn were behind a group of other men that were chained together, was a walk that could only be carried out carefully and slowly. As a result, it took almost half an hour for them to reach the gatehouse of the convict establishment.

Back in Britain, when Daniel had first set his eyes on Chatham Gaol, he had been struck by its splendid architecture. This time, as the sight of the gaol came into view, he was left open-mouthed and even more astounded at the sight of this impressive building towering before him. He assumed it had been designed to strike awe and fear into those about to be imprisoned within its walls. But if this was so, it wasn't having the desired effect on Daniel, as he felt more appreciative towards its bright white limestone design than had been otherwise intended.

There was a large gatehouse at the front, with two angled towers either side of an arched doorway. This reminded Daniel of those medieval castles he'd seen pictures of in books.

Above the doorway was a large black-faced clock with Roman numerals. Looking beyond the gatehouse, he could see the main prison block. This was a long, magnificent-looking building, also made from local white limestone, with long rows of windows, four storeys high. He correctly assumed that behind one of those windows, was a cell waiting for him.

Daniel glanced back towards the clock. Nudging a convict in a group next to him, he quipped, 'Hope they hurry up and get us inside or we might miss breakfast. I've heard they do a particularly nice dish of gruel here.'

No reply was forthcoming, but he could tell by the returned glare, this convict was in no mood to join in with the joke.

Daniel was with the first group of convicts taken through the large gatehouse, across the parade ground, and into the administration block. Once again he was made to go through a rigorous checking-in process. He was made to strip naked, and his body was carefully checked for anything dangerous that might have been hidden. This was followed by an examination for any moles, tattoos, marks, or disfigurements, which were then noted. Finally, he had his height measured, which was written down, along with the colour of his eyes and hair.

Daniel still found this process unpleasant, and even though he had gone through it several times now, he still found it humiliating. However, the hardest thing of all he encountered during the administration process at Fremantle, was having his name taken away from him. From now on, he would be known only as Convict Number 9263.

Having his body thoroughly inspected was one thing, but the complete removal of his name hit him extremely hard. His whole identity had now been removed, and throughout the next two weeks he suffered many deep waves of insecurity because of it. Although, as time moved on, he found himself becoming accustomed to it, or at least subconsciously ignoring it.

After this part of the process had been completed, he was ordered to dress, then taken to another part of the prison, where he was given a plate, mug, toothbrush, and a new full set of clothing. This was the prisoners' summer issue, which included a jacket, waistcoat, duck trousers, four cotton shirts, two neckerchiefs, socks, a felt cap, and a new pair of boots. Having all these things given to him made Daniel feel as if many of his birthdays had all come at once. Back home, just to have been given one of these items would have been a happy event, but none more so than the new pair of boots.

With his new kit in arms, Daniel was taken away to his new cell. This appeared little different to all those he had been placed in before. Just seven feet long, four feet wide, with a hammock tied at one end to the outer wall, and the other end attached to a bracket by the door. Almost touching the side of the hammock was a small collapsible table, fixed to the side wall. High up on the outer wall was a small, barred window. This could be slightly opened, allowing a little fresh air to enter what would otherwise be an unbearably stifling cell. Especially in this land of much warmer, sunnier weather than Britain had usually provided. As the door slammed behind him, the relative freedom of the past two months on board ship already seemed a distant memory. Leaning against the side of his cell, he slowly lowered himself down onto the floor. He settled himself, put his head in his hands, and closed his eyes, attempting to block out the deluge of thoughts which were now spinning around his mind. Mostly thoughts of spending the next few years of his life without being able to use his name. It was as if he was now going to be treated like an animal, no longer a person. Although even a dog would be given a name. A dark wave of gloom came over him as he huddled up into a ball on the floor.

Fortunately it wasn't long before he fell fast asleep, giving him a much-needed escape from the danger of completely breaking down.

The next three months followed the similar regimented, monotonous daily drag, the same as he had encountered back in Aylesbury and Chatham. He felt that he should have been used to it by now, but, having spent the past two months with the considerable freedom he had enjoyed on the *Corona*, it took some getting used to.

It was the same old familiar sound of bells going off for every event. Although here in Fremantle the wake-up bell varied between 5 a.m. And 6 a.m., according to the time of year. Unfortunately as it was now December, and therefore summertime, the wake-up bell rang at 5 a.m. Another bell sounded at 5.55 a.m. for the day's work to commence, and shortly before 8 a.m. another bell sounded for everyone to stop for breakfast. This mainly consisted of bread and black tea. It was then back to work until lunchtime, which was at midday, and would include things such as bread, soup or gruel, steamed meat, and vegetables.

The convicts were only issued with one bowl, which would be needed for the soup or gruel, so Daniel had no choice other than to use his dirty towel to hold the meat or bread in. Daniel noticed with his first serving that it had a slightly better taste than he had to put up with back at Chatham. The portions dished out had increased too, especially the chunks of meat or cheese. It wasn't a great deal more, but certainly an increase, and it was gratefully received.

After dinner there was still more work to be done, which continued until 6 p.m. when Daniel would have a rushed wash before supper. This would consist of yet more bread, along with either tea or cocoa. The day finally ended with prayers in the chapel, at 6.45 p.m., then returning to his cell by 8 p.m., ready for lights out.

On Daniel's second day at Fremantle, he was pleased to be visited by the prison's chaplain, the Reverend Richard Alderson. Daniel had assumed there would be a man of the cloth at the establishment, and he had meant to ask the religious instructor on board the *Corona* if this would be the case, but he never got round to it.

Back in Great Hadham, Daniel had attended church most Sundays with his family. He would usually listen intently to the sermons being preached and enjoy singing some of the hymns. Especially rousing ones such as 'Amazing Grace'. He would also join in with the prayers, led by the rector, but he wasn't usually given to praying at other times. However, since his visits from the religious instructor at Chatham, and from the Reverend Williams on board the *Corona*, his interest in the things of God had become increasingly important to him. Indeed, most nights he would try to say a short prayer before going to sleep, and it wasn't unknown for him to take to prayer during the daytime either. Especially if he found himself with a specific need.

Strangely though, he found it almost impossible to pray when he was going through the particularly dark periods of his life. Periods which often reared their ugly head throughout his time in gaol. He couldn't understand why it was, that in such times of deep depression, and when he probably needed it the most, he felt unable to pray. But he assumed that was probably just the nature of this depressive beast.

During his first visit, the Reverend Alderson informed Daniel that he'd received a very favourable report from the Reverend Williams regarding his overall conduct on the *Corona* and the tasks he'd undertaken. Daniel was delighted to hear this, as he knew the report would have also been passed on to the superintendent of the prison, which might be of benefit to him in the future.

The Reverend Alderson also mentioned that the Reverend Williams had spoken of the many meetings and conversations that had taken place between them during the voyage, especially regarding matters of faith. News of this had obviously impressed the Reverend Alderson, as he made it known to Daniel that he too would be most willing, should Daniel wish, to visit his cell when needed or even on a regular basis, perhaps once a week, to offer him some additional religious support. This was an offer Daniel gladly accepted, not only because he was genuinely interested in exploring his increasing faith in God, but he was also well aware that the Reverend Alderson would be keeping a written character report on him. So accepting this offer could potentially help his cause in other ways too!

As the Reverend Alderson was about to leave on that first visit, Daniel asked if he could have a Bible to read. The Reverend Alderson glanced over to the table in Daniel's cell saying, 'Oh, I'm sorry, there should already have been one there for you. Every cell should have one. I will bring one tomorrow.'

Daniel wasn't a fast reader, but he was literate, and he figured that having a Bible to read would not only help him learn more about the things that Jesus had done, but it would also help him more generally with his reading and spelling. Something he felt would be of help after he'd gained his freedom.

To Daniel's delight, the Reverend Alderson returned as promised with a cell Bible, and a smaller one, which he gifted to Daniel as one that he could keep for all time. He also brought with him a hard-backed book from the prison library called *The Christian Reader*. This was a religious teaching book, which had apparently been used at schools in America. Before leaving, the Reverend Alderson suggested that Daniel start by reading the Gospel of Matthew, which was the first book in the New Testament section of the Bible.

That evening, Daniel did as had been suggested. Not only did he read it that night, but almost every night for the remainder of his time in gaol. Indeed, he made it his aim to read at least one small piece of the Bible each night, for the rest of his life.

On his third day at Fremantle, Daniel was put to work inside the prison, spending most of the day on cleaning duties. It was work he didn't mind, but he seemed to spend most of his first two weeks in Fremantle tasked with this type of work, and he longed to be outside, even if it meant labouring on one of the many public works projects which were being carried out.

After two weeks of working within the prison walls, Daniel was eventually placed on a working party outside. At first he was in a chain gang. This mainly involved working on one of the roads not too far from the prison. It was very much hard labour, but it did have a good side to it as well. For he enjoyed being outside, especially in the warm fresh air, and it was also a little easier to grab the odd word of secret chatter with other convicts.

On the downside, having to carry out the work in leg chains was exceptionally difficult, and often very painful. So much so, that despite wearing gaiters to protect his legs, he soon started getting terrible sores and needed to be seen by the establishment's doctor, who at once confined Daniel to his cell.

This was not an opportunity for him to rest though; he faced three full days with laborious tasks to complete inside his cell. When he was deemed to have made 'sufficient' improvement, he was made to hobble along to one of the workshops to carry out tasks there. Mostly this would involve sitting on a hard wooden bench, picking oakum.

Being part of a chain gang was usually reserved for convicts who had misbehaved or were considered to be convicts who were likely to abscond. Daniel was confused as to why he had been placed in a chain gang, given his compliant character since his arrest. He wondered if his openness in saying that he wanted to be transported had been disbelieved, and he was only bluffing to aid an escape attempt. On the other hand, he wondered if his attachment to a chain gang had been an administrative error. Whatever it was, he dared not question why, and quietly accepted it.

To his immense relief, once his legs had recovered, he never returned to the chain gang, but was put with unchained working parties. Although this did not stop him suffering from further injuries. Following a stumble, while digging a roadside ditch, he sustained several nasty cuts, bruises, and strains to the muscles in his right arm, left leg, and back. Strangely, this turned out to be a blessing in disguise, with fortunes soon turning in his favour. On his recovery, Daniel was sent to work on the final construction stages of a new bridge.

His work here no longer involved days on end digging or heavy lifting, as most of this type of work had already been completed. Thankfully Daniel was given fairly light duties to carry out there, which greatly helped in aiding a full recovery.

He only worked on the bridge for a few weeks, but as his work there was far less physical, it came as a welcome relief. Working on the bridge also resulted in him gaining a very different kind of benefit too. A leaving gift.

The man in overall charge of the project was so delighted with all that 'he' had accomplished that he organised for all convicts involved in its construction to receive extra food rations. So, although only having been there for a few weeks, Daniel's name had been included in the list of those to benefit.

During his time engaged on various working parties, Daniel endeavoured to do all he could to be seen to follow the rules and would attempt to do everything ordered of him. He found this hard at times but would try the best he could not to upset the guards, either deliberately or otherwise. He was often tempted to give out a bit of backchat or a snarky comment, but he always managed to hold his tongue, or at least mutter it under his breath.

It was during his incarceration in Aylesbury that he first decided that this was the best course for him to take. A vow which he renewed on arrival at Chatham. Now, in Fremantle, he was even more aware that he couldn't afford to let this slip. If anything, he needed to make an even greater effort, and be even more resolute in keeping to it. His new determination was partly due to the bad marks which he understood could be handed out for such simple things as singing or swearing. These marks would be added up at the end of his sentence, and if he had collected too many, extra days could be added to his time.

There were apparently good marks to be earned too. He wasn't sure how these could be achieved, or even if they really existed, but there was always hope that if he was to be issued with some, his sentence would be reduced.

It was also the harshness of the various punishments, especially for more serious offences, that encouraged Daniel to endeavour to keep within the rules. Indeed it was shortly after his arrival, while taking his weekly bath, that he caught sight of another convict's back which was covered in large, raised scars. He later learned the convict had once tried to escape.

He had been working as part of a chain gang, but his leg chains had been removed in order to carry out some other duties, which couldn't be done while in chains. He had been working free from chains for a few hours when he saw a brief opportunity to make a run for it ... and he did. He managed to get several hundred yards before being spotted, which was actually quite a feat as he was wearing the distinctive yellow-and-black-squared 'magpie' uniform, which convicts who had previously misbehaved were usually made to wear.

Despite having run some distance, the uniform achieved what it was intended for, and he was easily spotted and recaptured. As a result of his escape attempt, he was sentenced to solitary confinement, having only bread and water for thirty days. During this time he was also ordered to be given one hundred lashes. The convict passed out after receiving fewer than twenty lashes on the first administration of these, so he was dragged back to his cell to recover. This happened on two other days, until he had received the full one hundred lashes.

Although this kind of punishment, and the sight of the scars received by escapees, worked in deterring most convicts from attempting any escape, there were still those who got to a point where they couldn't bear any more of the prison regime or lack of freedom. So it wasn't uncommon for a convict to try and make a break for it, either by running into the bush or jumping into the river.

CHAPTER 21

The Association Ward

Almost a year to the day after arriving at the convict establishment, Daniel received some wonderful news.

It was early in the morning, and he was standing by his cell door, waiting as usual for a warder to release him. First he would need to slop out before quickly making his way over to the exercise yard for roll call. Once that had been completed, the day's work would begin.

Daniel heard the key turning in the lock and watched as the cell door opened. However, this time, and quite unexpectedly, along with the prison warder entered the Reverend Alderson. Without even a hello, he said, 'I have some news for you. You'll be pleased to hear I had a meeting yesterday with the superintendent. He's informed me you'll soon to be moved to the association ward, in preparation for receiving your ticket-of-leave.'

Daniel could hardly believe what he was hearing, beaming the biggest smile he'd achieved in a very long time.

'When will I be moved?' he asked.

'I believe it may be later this week. It's also my understanding that if you continue with your good form, you could be ready to receive your ticket before Easter.'

Daniel's eyes started to water, and a tear began to trickle down his cheek as an emotional wave of excitement welled up from within. This was yet another step towards his freedom. A move to the association ward meant he would no longer be in a cell but would be sleeping in an open dormitory. Furthermore, within a few months he could be enjoying even greater freedom, with a ticket-of-leave in his pocket.

He was under no misconceptions, though. He knew that having his ticket didn't mean having full freedom. But at least he would be free to find work and accommodation outside of the prison's confines.

Daniel wiped the tear away. 'Sorry, sir,' he said with an embarrassed mumble.

'Keep strong, man,' replied the Reverend, then added, 'You must remember that your ticket-of-leave has a lot of conditions attached. It isn't your conditional release or ticket of freedom. That can only come after your seven-year sentence has been completed.'

Daniel took a deep breath, managing to control his emotions before answering him. 'Yes, sir, I am fully aware of that, but thank you for reminding me … Although it is such a big step towards my freedom, isn't it?'

'Indeed it is. But make sure you don't falter now.' The Reverend clasped his hands together. 'I must be on my way. I have a lot of work to attend to, and so do you. However, before I go, may I pray that God will help you to keep your feet firmly on the right road?'

Daniel nodded his approval at the offer and glanced towards the warder for affirmation, which was given.

Daniel then bowed his head as the Reverend commenced a short prayer. After he had finished with the usual 'Amen', he left the cell, leaving Daniel standing, staring into nowhere, with the wonderful news he'd just been given ringing in his ears.

The warder didn't allow him any more time with his thoughts and gave his upper arm a slight shake to bring him back to where he was. A stark reminder that he did indeed have a day's hard labouring ahead of him.

It was only two days later when Daniel was moved to the association ward – a communal living area at the far end of the cell block. Things were run a lot differently there, with just the one warder in charge. Although he would always be firm, keeping strict order, a lot more fairness and humanity was now shown to the convicts. This was something which Daniel noticed within hours of being moved. Probably due to the fact that he'd rarely experienced this since his first day of confinement in Hertford Gaol.

For the next two months Daniel ate and slept in the association ward, along with around fifty other convicts. Most of them, like Daniel, were being prepared for release with their ticket-of-leave in pocket. There were three convicts on the ward who had already received their ticket, but up to that point had been unable to find anyone to employ them. There were also one or two men who, although they had managed to find work, hadn't yet received their first wage, so had been unable to rent a room near their place of work. Because of their situation, they were permitted to continue staying in the association ward until such time as they could find, and pay for, some form of accommodation.

CHAPTER 22

Ticket-of-Leave

1 February 1868

Daniel and his fellow convicts in the association ward had finished their breakfast, cleaned up, and were standing in two lines ready to be escorted outside for the second stint of the day's labour.

As they were waiting, two warders entered the room and began speaking to the warder in charge. Following a short conversation between them, the warder in charge turned and scanned the rows of convicts, until arriving at Daniel.

'9263, come here.'

Daniel's heart began pounding as he made his way over towards the group of warders. He couldn't think of any reason for being singled out. As far as he knew, he hadn't knowingly disobeyed any rules, and was sure his ticket-of-leave wouldn't be coming his way for several more weeks. He had almost reached them when one of the warders who had just come in stepped forward and addressed Daniel.

'You're to come with me to the superintendent's

office.'

'Why is that, sir? I've not done wrong, have I?' replied Daniel with a nervous wobble.

The warder gave a humorous snort. 'Don't fret, man. It's your lucky day – you're getting your ticket-of-leave.'

Daniel couldn't believe what he had just heard. 'I'm sorry, sir, w-what did you say?' he stuttered.

The warder didn't directly answer Daniel's question, but said, 'Come on, follow me ... If you want it, that is,' and proceeded to march out of the ward at a pace.

Daniel looked towards his fellow convicts, gave them a massive grin, raised his fist in triumph, and scurried out of the room as fast as he could.

During his time on the association ward, Daniel had been informed by those in authority and had gleaned a few other bits of information by hearsay about the ticket-of-leave system. Things such as how and where to go to find work, where he might find lodgings, and to make sure that he had his ticket with him at all times. He also knew that he was never to be disruptive or aggressive, and certainly never to be found drunk. Breaking one of these, or any of the other rules laid down, would result in completing the remainder of his sentence back behind the walls of Fremantle Gaol.

As he walked along the prison corridors, heading out of the cell block for what he hoped would be the last time, his cheerful mood changed and he began feeling mightily concerned about his imminent release, and what this new phase in his life was about to bring.

It began to dawn on Daniel that he had just spent the past four years of his life having his every basic need provided for. Food, clothing, and shelter. But now that he was about to begin life in the outside world once again, he would need to find all these basic necessities for himself.

A wave of panic began to overwhelm him. Would he be able to find work? What would happen if he fell sick and couldn't work? What if he didn't earn enough money to buy enough food to live on?

So many questions began swirling around his head. Over the past few years he'd dreamed of a multitude of things which he'd gain once issued with his ticket-of- leave. Now, try as he might, he was unable to bring any of these things to mind. All he could think of were the countless problems that were, potentially, in store for him.

On approaching the steps to the governor's office, the irony of how he was now feeling began to break through all his panic, enabling his special wry grin to appear once again.

He began recalling all the years of suffering he'd gone through. Things ranging from the painful, mindless turning of the crank, to the digging of roadside ditches. He also remembered the years of being unable to converse freely with those around him, and of course having his name removed. Because of these things, and more, he'd not only suffered physically but also mentally. Enduring countless waves of deep, dark depression that had engulfed his innermost being. On occasions this had caused him to completely give up, but somehow he always managed to hang on, even though at times it was by the skin of his teeth.

As the superintendent's office came insight, Daniel thought it slightly strange that, having survived all of this, and having seen many events unexpectedly working in his favour during this time, he was still worrying about what may or may not happen in the future. He also knew that his leaving prison, and facing life in the outside world again, was a necessary journey. One which he had to undertake in order to reach his dream.

The warder knocked on the door of the office, and on hearing the reply to enter, he began to steadily open it. The door had opened but a few inches when Daniel noticed the superintendent wasn't alone in the room. Standing with him was the Reverend Alderson. Daniel hadn't expected to see him there – he had no reason to. But Daniel was pleased, as he would have the opportunity to thank the Reverend for all of the spiritual guidance and comfort that he'd given Daniel since his arrival at Fremantle.

The superintendent stood up, addressing Daniel with a short speech. This was mainly a reminder of why he had been locked up in the first place, and the numerous rules and regulations he needed to abide by whilst away from the prison. The superintendent had obviously given this speech many times before, as it was said without any feeling, or change in tone, and was delivered as if reading from a book.

Having said his piece, he sat down again, in his plush padded-leather desk chair, which stood behind a large, very ornately carved wooden desk. He turned towards the Reverend, but speaking to Daniel, said, 'Now, the Reverend Alderson has something he would like to tell you.'

Daniel gave a friendly smile of recognition towards the Reverend, which wasn't returned as he had already begun to speak ...

'On a number of occasions you've told me that you felt unable to repent of your crime, as you believed it was the only way out of the situation you were in. We still differ in this conclusion; nevertheless, I am heartened by the fact that you accept your actions caused inconvenience to many, and much distress to your family, too. I also acknowledge that many a man would have held on to this view, but in order to deceive me, would have displayed a sense of false remorse. This you have not done ... So, regardless of lack of remorse, I believe you to be an honest man, with a growing godly faith. A faith which I hope you will take with you as you go from this place.'

The Reverend paused, tilting his head a little, giving a glance towards Daniel as if seeking a response. Daniel replied with a slow thoughtful nod of his head.

Satisfied with this, the Reverend continued to deliver some good news.

'Now, I am not usually given to doing such a thing for convicts, but I have taken the liberty of organising for you a position of employment, as a labourer on a new section of road which is being constructed just outside Perth.'

'Wow, that's most kind of you, Reverend. I am most grateful,' said Daniel.

'And I have some more good news for you,' replied the Reverend. He left a short, tantalising pause before continuing. 'I have an acquaintance, a Mr Holt, and his wife. Both are godly people, and regular members of a church in Perth. I've told them of your character, and they are happy for you to rent a small lodge from them. It's located beside their house. The rent will be no more than you would need to pay for a single room elsewhere in the area, and Mr Holt has also informed me that you may stay there for the first month without any charge.'

Daniel shook his head in disbelief on hearing what the Reverend was saying, and was completely lost for words. The Reverend could see this was the case, so didn't wait for a response, but continued giving Daniel a little more information.

'You are to start work this very morning, and at the end of the day you are to make your way to Mr Holt's home, where you will introduce yourself to him.'

Daniel was astounded at all he had been told. It was as though he was living in some kind of dream, yet at the same time knew this was for real. 'I thank you from the bottom of my heart, for all you've done for me previously. I don't know how I could ever repay you,' he said.

The Reverend replied, in a way that only a reverend could, 'By henceforth living a godly, upright life. I'm sure this would be enough to satisfy me, and to have made my efforts more than worthwhile.'

'I will endeavour to do that,' replied Daniel and, offering his hand towards the Reverend, he said, 'May I shake your hand, sir?'

He opened his hand in return, and Daniel moved forward, shaking his hand firmly. The Reverend then removed from his pocket a piece of paper and, handing it to Daniel, said, 'I have written down your place of work, and the name of the clerk for the works. It is he you must report to on your arrival … underneath that is the address of Mr Holt.'

Daniel took the piece of paper, glanced at what was written on it, and kissed it, before placing it firmly and deeply into his pocket for safety.

The superintendent rose from his chair once again to give his final address to Daniel.

'You will now go with the warder to the stores. There you will receive a new set of clothes and be met by a Pensioner Guard, who will escort you to your new place of work.'

He handed Daniel a few official-looking papers, then in an exceptionally strict tone said, 'Now, remember ... As Reverend Alderson has just reminded you, this is only your ticket-of-leave. So during this next period of your life you must comply with the rules. A copy of which I have also handed to you. If you break any of these, you will find yourself back in here, without delay.'

This change in the superintendent's tone brought Daniel back down to earth with a bang. Having just received such good news, he had momentarily forgotten the fact that he wasn't being completely set free. Nevertheless, he was still buoyed by the thought that he would soon be working in a job without guards observing his every move. He would also be able to change jobs whenever he wanted, if he could find another one, that was. But right now, the best thing of all was that he had somewhere to live and would never need to spend another night locked in a prison cell ever again.

Another benefit he was greatly looking forward to was being able to meet and talk with other people without restriction, as long as this didn't involve the drinking of too much alcohol. Something which was prohibited under his terms of release.

As Daniel left the office, making his way towards the stores, his memory drifted back to that unforgettable day in Chatham Gaol. The time when he was at his very lowest, and saw the rainbow through the workroom window.

But he was still under no illusion, fully accepting

he'd not yet reached the end of his rainbow. However, he was uplifted by the fact that it was coming ever closer. He was also feeling increasingly confident that one day the rainbow would not only be within touching distance, but he may also be able to hold that pot of gold at the bottom of it.

CHAPTER 23

Goodbye Fremantle

An hour after entering the superintendent's office, Daniel was finally leaving Fremantle Gaol for what he hoped would be the last time. He was being accompanied by Mr Attwood, a Pensioner Guard who had arrived a year before Daniel on a convict ship called, *Racehorse*.

Their paths had crossed on many occasions during Daniel's time at Fremantle, mainly when he'd been working in the prison workshops. During their encounters he had witnessed Mr Attwood's firmness but had never marked him down as a particularly unjust guard.

The morning's weather was gloriously pleasant and sunny, with a light breeze blowing in from the sea, which pleased Daniel as it would help make the day's work a little more tolerable. Something he knew would be essential if he was to put on a good show during his first day on site.

Daniel had walked less than fifty yards from the gates when he began glaring down towards his boots, becoming a little angry with himself at the way he was now behaving. He was taking small shuffling steps, with his head bowed and hands together in front of him as if holding a chain, but he wasn't. He couldn't believe he was still behaving, albeit unconsciously, in this 'convict' manner.

While he was admonishing himself for this action, he also became aware of the amusing side of it, and murmured to himself, 'You stupid fool, the chains are gone, never to be put on again.'

With that, he stood tall, put his arms out wide, and raised his head towards the sky. In the process of doing this, he found himself glancing towards the guard, slightly concerned this would be deemed as some sort of improper behaviour. Fortunately for Daniel, the guard grinned, which gave Daniel a greater feeling of confidence. Emboldened by this, and with his arms still open, he began spinning round, while making sure he didn't hit the guard with either his arms or the canvas bag that was hanging over his shoulder. This bag now contained all his worldly possessions, his plate, mug, a few extra clothes, and the Bible which had been given to him by the Reverend Alderson.

After three turns Daniel stopped, and he attempted to test the boundaries of his new-found freedom further by saying something to the guard. But as his mouth opened, he was unable to think of anything to say. For years he'd been forced to undertake almost everything he did in silence, so this had now become the natural thing for him to do. An idea for something to say popped into his head. He could ask how long it would take to reach the works. But before he was able to say anything, more doubts crept in, convinced that conversation between the two of them would be a step too far at this point, so he continued walking in silence, deciding to wait until spoken to first.

They were heading down to the harbourside to take an open carriage into Perth. During the walk to the harbour, Daniel found himself surveying the land around, engrossed with everything that was in view. He had walked this route many times before, on his way to and from various working duties. However, right now he was seeing everything from a brand-new perspective. It was as if he was setting his eyes upon everything around him for the very first time.

The silence between himself and Mr Attwood remained until they had climbed on board the carriage, when the silence was soon broken. 'Where do you come from, Daniel?' asked the guard, startling Daniel in the process.

'I come from ...' Daniel stopped, taken aback at what he had just heard. Not only had he been asked a question about his personal life, and seemingly out of interest, he'd also been called by his name, not a number. The Reverend Alderson had occasionally called him by name, probably unintentionally, but hearing a guard addressing him in such a way seemed out of place, even wrong. But it wasn't, and for the first time in many years, he was no longer a number. He was once again

Daniel. Daniel Phillips.

'I come from Great Hadham, a village in Hertfordshire, sir,' he eventually replied.

'Oh, I've never been to Hertfordshire. I was brought up in Somerset, and Gloucestershire. After that I went to India.'

'India, wow. Why were you there?' asked Daniel.

'I was a corporal, in the 66th Regiment of Foot.'

'Sounds great, but not the life for me though,' replied Daniel, and they carried on talking, covering a vast array of subjects as they went. Subjects ranging from Daniel's home life, and his misdemeanour there, to general events that had taken place back in Britain and throughout the empire.

For the first time in four years, Daniel was able to talk at length, indulging in general discussions without care. He had of course conversed with the religious instructors, which was much appreciated, but he still had to be guarded with the things he would say. But right now, here he was, talking with a Pensioner Guard without any caution, and enjoying every moment of it.

One forever memorable part of their conversation was hearing the news that only two more shipments of convicts had taken place after his own arrival. Furthermore, there were not to be any others. Of the last two transportations, one had been in 1867, the year following Daniel's arrival, and the last shipment had only landed the previous month.

Daniel couldn't believe how lucky he was to have

made it onto the *Corona* when he did. He was fairly certain the authorities wouldn't have sent him on any of those last two shipments, as by that time he'd have spent so much time in Chatham that he'd have almost been due his ticket-of-leave anyway. He knew he'd made it by the narrowest of margins.

CHAPTER 24

A New Job, a New Abode

From Perth, Daniel and Mr Attwood had quite a walk ahead of them, but eventually the works depot came into view, and with it, Mr Attwood's demeanour began to change a little. The relaxed, personal conversations waned, and any talk was kept to reminders on how he was to behave in the future.

Having spent this time chatting, almost as if he was a friend, seeing him revert back to a Pensioner Guard was a little disconcerting. However, Daniel perfectly understood the reason why he was behaving this way, so went along with it.

The situation reminded him of the time when he was first arrested, and the manner in which Constable Newland had been with him until Inspector Ryder arrived to take him away.

Daniel and Mr Attwood reached the works depot, and after much enquiring as to the whereabouts of the clerk of the works, Mr Passmore, they eventually found him, but then had a long wait before he had time to deal with them.

There were the usual official things to go

through, such as the details of where Daniel would be staying while under his employment, more repeated instructions regarding the rules of his ticket, and the regulations to abide by on site.

By the time all the formalities had been completed, it was early afternoon, so the clerk of works suggested to Daniel that he should report for his first day's work the following morning. This suggestion was gratefully accepted, as the day had been rather draining for Daniel in so many ways. The journey to the works in itself had been physically tiring, but having to deal with all the differing waves of emotions which had come his way that morning had left him mentally exhausted too. In addition to all of this, he knew there would be more of this to follow once he'd arrived at his new home.

Before departing, Daniel and Mr Attwood were invited to go to the canteen tent, where they were given a mug of tea, and a little bread and cheese to help them on their way. While they were eating, Mr Attwood mentioned that he was familiar with the area where Daniel would be staying, and he offered to escort him over to the house. An offer Daniel was more than pleased to accept.

Almost as soon as they had left the depot, the conversation between them became more friendly again, and in little over half an hour they had arrived at Mr Holt's home.

As Daniel went to knock on the door, he hesitated. Once again he was in a situation where everything seemed so unreal. It had been many years since he had done such a simple thing as knocking on the door of a house.

Mr Attwood looked at Daniel, and without waiting for Daniel to knock, he tapped on the door with the back of his hand. It appeared that Mr Holt had seen them approaching, for as soon as the first knock sounded, the door opened. Daniel introduced himself and Mr Attwood, Mr Holt did the same, and they were both warmly welcomed into his home.

In no time at all they were sitting down in comfy armchairs, partaking of a freshly brewed pot of tea and a small selection of sandwiches, filled with either chicken, cheese, or honey.

If only my mother could see me now, thought Daniel, as he took the first bite from his honey sandwich. *I'm sure she'd be pleased things were turning out so well for me … At least I hope so.*

Having finished his tea, Mr Attwood sought assurance from Mr and Mrs Holt that they were completely satisfied to have Daniel stay with them. Readily gaining it, he bade them all farewell and departed.

No sooner had the door shut behind him than Mrs Holt insisted on pouring another round of tea and encouraged Daniel to indulge in another sandwich, an offer he didn't hesitate to accept. Daniel then began telling them a little about himself, his home in Great Hadham, his family, and the events which led to him firing the stack.

After Daniel had brought them up to date, Mr Holt got to his feet, to begin what was obviously a pre-thought-out welcome address. Mr Holt had intended to give his speech as soon as Daniel had arrived but, due to him arriving with an unexpected companion, had left it until now.

'So, Daniel, we are a God-fearing family here, and I understand from my friend, the Reverend Alderson, that you have a growing faith in God too ... I am aware that your ticket-of-leave rules insist you need to attend church. But I was most delighted to hear from the Reverend that you'll be doing so out of a desire, not by order.'

Daniel nodded his head in agreement, as Mr Holt continued, 'You are obviously at liberty to attend whichever church you wish in the area, but we would be most happy if you were to join with us at the church we attend. And after the Sunday services, you will be most welcome to come back and partake of lunch with us.' He glanced towards Mrs Holt then, turning his sight back towards Daniel, said, 'Obviously we are not your guardians, so will not be keeping an eye on your every move, and we don't want to interfere in how you live your life. You are simply renting accommodation from us. Having said that, we want you to know that you are most welcome to knock on our door at any time. Whether you be in need of something, or just want to talk. Loneliness can lead a man to drink, and destruction. I would not like to see you travel down that road, ending up back in trouble.'

'Oh, I am determined not to allow that to happen, sir,' interrupted Daniel.

As Daniel spoke, it dawned on Mr Holt that Daniel was probably unaware of their Christian names. He apologised, 'Oh, please forgive me. I formally introduced myself to you on the doorstep, but I think we can be a little less formal now ... My name is Charles, and this is my wife, Mahala.'

Daniel nodded towards them individually, saying their names in turn, as an acknowledgement of the invitation to call them by their Christian names.

Charles then continued, 'We wish to be here as your friends. We do not judge you for what you have done in the past, although you need to be aware that many folk in this town will judge you, and always have a distrust of you. You may not always find things easy here. There are those in this community, like ourselves, that are prepared to give you a chance, but...' he narrowed his eyes, considering what he was about to say, then said, 'I strongly advise you avoid mixing with ex-convicts in your social time. Not all of them will have changed their ways or be as determined as you are to walk along the straight and narrow path. Things will be tough for you here, and during those difficult times one can be easily led astray. So with that in mind, and if you are content for me to do so, I will try to help you by introducing you to some fair-minded folk in whom I trust, and think will be a good influence on you.' Charles glanced at his fob watch. 'Well, I think that I've said enough for now, other than to repeat, you are most welcome to call on us at any time for help, advice, or anything else you may require.'

Charles sat back down, and with it, Daniel rose, feeling it appropriate to respond to the warm welcome by standing, even though he was unsure what he was going to say. A simple 'thank you' was certainly far too inadequate, especially given the welcome he'd just received. Also, having spent most of his time over the past few years having limited opportunities to talk with others, he was rather out of practice with the art, and he felt anxious that any words about to depart from his mouth would not reflect the gratitude he felt for the Holts' generosity towards him.

Daniel slowly rubbed his chin, giving himself a little more time to compose himself. He figured the only option available would be to start with a simple thank you, then hopefully that would lead him on to say a little more. To say nothing, now that he was standing, clearly wasn't an option, so he began.

'Thank you, sir ... I mean Charles, and indeed to you, Mahala, for your most kind welcome, the offers, and sound advice to me. Advice which I will endeavour to follow. And yes, I'd welcome any introduction to such folk whom you think fit. All this wonderful hospitality you've bestowed on me is greatly appreciated, and I'll do everything possible to ensure that all you've done will not be wasted.' As he said this, he began feeling a little overwhelmed with everything. He wanted to say more, but fearing his emotions were about to get the better of him, and feeling a little self-conscious, he sat back down.

Mahala, sensing Daniel's discomfort, quickly interjected, 'Oh, I am perfectly sure that our hospitality will not be wasted.' She then began gathering up the empty cups, adding, 'I'll just take these into the kitchen. Then I think it's time we showed you to your room.'

Daniel smiled, repeating those last words in his head. *To your room.* It sounded so good. No longer was he going to be spending the night in a cell – he was going to be in a room.

His memory flew back to that occasion in the past when he'd been determined to look upon his cell as a room instead of as a cell. He never really succeeded in convincing himself of this, and his initial determination had slipped by the way a long time ago, but it certainly helped him get through that initial period.

Even though Mahala had called his accommodation a room, it was more than that; it was a reasonably sized single-room lodge. Far better than any room in a house could ever have been for him, and he was well aware that few 'ticket' convicts, if any, would ever have had the privilege of staying in such a place.

That night, Daniel lay down in a nice warm comfortable bed for the first time in many years. A far cry from the hammocks, hard thin lumpy mattresses, or those boards supplied in Aylesbury Gaol.

Daniel studied his room with a massive smile of contentment. It was many times larger than the tiny cells in which he'd been locked up over the past few years, and some four times larger than the bedroom he'd shared with his brother back in Great Hadham.

The place was well furnished too, with a chest of drawers, wardrobe, small dining table, and a wooden chair. There was a small stove, with several pots and pans hanging on the wall above it, and at the other end of the room was the bed that he was now lying in.

Above his bed hung two oil paintings. A small still-life painting of a bowl of fruit, and beside it was a larger painting, of what could best be described as a typical English country landscape. Sheep grazing in a meadow beside a ripe cornfield, and a range of hills and trees in the distance. Seeing this painting filled Daniel with mixed emotions. A number of happy memories came flooding back of lovely summer days that he'd enjoyed back in Great Hadham with his family and friends. At the same time, those memories left him with twinges of homesickness. He also found it rather poignant that the painting included a ripe cornfield, which would always be there as a constant reminder of his past act.

At one side of his bed there was an old but comfy armchair, perfect for him to recline in after he'd returned from work each evening. On the other side was a small bamboo-framed table, covered with a lace cloth. On top stood a small oil lamp and a Bible. Underneath was a small shelf with two books on top of each other. One was a book on household management, which Daniel didn't even bother to open as he felt this type of reading would be more suited to that of a lady than himself. The other seemed to be a children's book, about an adventure a little girl called Alice had taken. This didn't sound at all interesting to him, in fact it seemed a little childish, but he did eventually read it, finding it rather strange but surprisingly enjoyable.

He placed the Bible underneath the table with the other two books, as he still had his own, special Bible, which had been given to him by the Reverend Alderson. This was now given pride of place on top of the table.

This accommodation wasn't simply a room for Daniel, it was a home. He was determined to do everything possible to ensure he'd never lose it and end up back in prison. He closed his eyes, whispering to himself, 'I am free.' But in saying this, he was still very conscious of the fact that he wasn't completely free, and still had many restrictions to adhere too.

Daniel also realised that in the morning he would be off to work. From bitter past experience, he knew that working on the roads wasn't an easy task, and he needed to work well at all times, as this would be crucial in keeping his employment, and his new home.

He began to feel a little nervous, having all sorts of thoughts about his new job. Fortunately, before he had dwelt too long on these fears, another joyous thought came to him ... He'd no longer be made to get up so early each morning. In fact, he would be staying in bed for over an hour longer. Daniel gave a long, contented sigh, and very soon fell asleep, enjoying his best night's sleep in years.

CHAPTER 25

Making Friends

For the next two weeks, and as expected, Daniel's work mainly involved the digging of ditches along the roadside or shifting gravel and stones. All the same type of work he'd experienced for days on end since his arrival at Fremantle Gaol.

The work was still just as physical as before, but with one major difference. This time, there were no guards watching his every move, shouting at him for taking a quick breather or talking to other workmates. There were guards around, of course. Many of whom he knew from his time spent on the working parties. But now, these guards were keeping an eye on the convicts still serving time, instead of him. Daniel would often show a smug grin when he was having a casual chat with a workmate and a guard passed by, knowing full well they could no longer reprimand him for doing such a thing. However, he was only too aware that if he did anything untoward against his ticket-of-leave conditions, the guards were at liberty to drag him back to prison once again – and they would probably take great pleasure in doing so.

Daniel regularly found himself working alongside groups of convicts. He recognised many of them and would love to have used his new-found freedom to converse with them. The problem in doing this would be that he'd not only get himself into hot water but would get the convicts into even greater trouble. So he tried to avoid being near them for too long, so as not to put either himself or the convicts in any compromising positions.

He was also able to appreciate why 'ticket' men had behaved in the same way towards himself while he was in convict uniform. In the past, he couldn't understand why they would snub his occasional, discreet attempts for a snatched moment of communication, but he now fully understood why this was.

Their rebuffs caused a lot of resentment from the convicts, who felt that the ticket men had become rather self-righteous and were looking down upon them. But now Daniel knew that this had never been the case. Nevertheless, he knew from experience how much it would mean to a convict if he were able to have a little communication with someone, however small it was. So during meal times, if he could be assured the guards were safely distracted, he would try and grab the occasional whispered word with a convict, knowing this would help lift their spirits, albeit for a brief moment.

***

Towards the end of his second month of working on the road-building project, Daniel managed to gain a welcome change to his employment. It all came about when Daniel was having his lunch with two other free workers.

He couldn't help but notice that things were significantly more hectic that day, and everything seemed rather more unorganised than was usually the case. It was clear, by the rather long time they had spent waiting for their food, that more workers were probably needed in both the kitchen and with carting refreshments to those who were a little too far from the eating area to be able to get to the canteen, eat, and get back in the time allotted.

This was the first time Daniel had met the two men that he was eating with, and during their introductions he learned that one of them was an ex-convict who had gained his freedom a few years earlier. The other was the son of a settler, who had come to Fremantle several decades beforehand.

At one point during their lunch break, Daniel commented about the long delay in getting their food. The ex-convict mentioned he'd heard whispers that three of the men who were usually involved in cooking the meals had been taken ill, and had been sent back home for fear of spreading the sickness throughout the workforce.

In a flash, Daniel could see this situation could well offer up a chance of gaining an easier placement. Even if it would only be for a day or two, it would come as a welcome break for him. So he quickly finished eating the rest of his meal, then casually made his way over to the tented kitchen, where he spotted a cook working inside.

He introduced himself and immediately noticed by the accent of the cook's response that he was probably from Yorkshire. Not really knowing how else to start up a conversation with this stranger, he decided, in good old English tradition, to mention the weather! He then managed, rather cunningly, to direct the conversation around to the fact that he'd worked with the cook on board the *Corona*. Also, that should the need ever arise, he would be willing to help out.

Fortunately for him, divulging this information had the desired effect, for in no time at all word had filtered its way back to the man in overall charge of the canteen area, and by the end of day Daniel was offered a job in the kitchen. An offer which he didn't hesitate to accept, and eagerly began working there the following day.

At this time, things were going extremely well for Daniel in all aspects of his life. All the other ticket-of-leave convicts he'd met were living in very small rented rooms. Daniel, on the other hand, was living what seemed to them, and indeed to himself, a life of luxury. Because of this, he soon learned not to let on to anyone about his good fortune, for fear of it causing resentment and animosity towards him.

Sunday mornings were spent at church with

Charles and Mahala. Following the service, he would usually enjoy the rest of the day by lunching with them. This tended to be in their home, but on nice sunny days they would go for a picnic.

Occasionally he would be invited to have lunch with some of the other families who attended the church. This was something he always appreciated, as it gave him the chance to widen his social circle of friends. Daniel enjoyed Charles and Mahala's company but, having been deprived of proper social contacts for several years, he wanted to enjoy as many folks' company as he could.

It was at the church when Daniel first met Mr and Mrs Baker, and their daughter Ruth.

The Baker family were close friends of Charles and Mahala, and often sat beside them in church. After the service had concluded, they would usually stay behind, talking with them at some length.

Mr Baker owned a nearby farm, and Ruth worked at a general store in Perth. Mr Baker had emigrated to the Swan River Colony around 1830. At the time he was just a young boy, and had arrived with his father, mother, sister, and some livestock. His father had been granted just over two hundred acres of land. Their initial excitement on arrival had been short-lived though, as they soon discovered the land was rather poor and his father was worried his sheep and cattle were not going to thrive there. So he sold most of the animals, replacing them with a large number of chickens. This decision proved to be very successful for his father, and by the time he had inherited the farm from him, they were not only selling eggs and chickens to the public in Perth and Fremantle, they were also supplying the convict establishment.

Mr Baker had been raised with the knowledge that his cousin Robert had been transported to Van Diemen's Land for sheep stealing. A crime which the family claimed he'd been completely innocent of. Although Daniel was never quite so sure about this!

Fortunately for Daniel, due to their family history and the alleged wrong conviction of his cousin, Mr Baker's family had been brought up with the attitude that convicts should all be given a second chance. All of this helped Daniel to feel quite at ease in their company.

CHAPTER 26

Romance in the Air

Ruth was a similar age to Daniel, and it wasn't long after their first introduction that they began spending ever more time chatting alone after the church service had finished. Ruth was always interested in hearing Daniel's tales of his time in gaol, and about his life in faraway Britain. She also hadn't failed to notice his charming smile and cheeky grin.

Daniel found Ruth very attractive too. Both in looks and with her quiet, unassuming personality. She was very gently spoken and, like Daniel, had a good sense of humour. Often, if she'd been amused by something, it would be expressed with an endearing giggle, while looking sidewards at the same time. A characteristic that he was especially drawn to.

Daniel soon started looking for any small excuse he could to justify making a visit to the store where Ruth worked. This would usually be on his way home, after his day's work, even though it was a little out of his way. He wasn't sure if it was just his imagination, but she appeared to make every effort to serve him before the owner of the store was able to. One thing he was certain of, though, she would always give him a nice smile when he left the store. Furthermore, her smile was always accompanied by her saying something like 'I hope I will see you soon' or 'I hope I will see you at church on Sunday'.

Once a month Daniel and the Holt and Baker families would have a picnic together after church. Mostly going to a secluded spot on the far part of the farm which Mr Baker owned. He had inherited the farm from his parents after they had sadly passed away within a year of each other.

These picnics served as a good opportunity for Daniel and Ruth to spend more time together, enabling their friendship to grow ever deeper. This blossoming relationship was becoming obvious to all around, even though Daniel and Ruth were oblivious of these observations.

Although Daniel was only lodging with Charles and Mahala, he had begun to look upon them as parent figures. They were comfortable with this and were more than happy to take him under their wing, as a parent would a son.

One day, as Daniel was returning from work, he saw Mahala taking washing off the line, which strung up in the garden between their two houses. He was pleased to see her, as he'd been hoping to bump into either her or Charles at some point, as he wanted to ask if he could call on them one evening for a bit of advice.

Daniel made his way over to Mahala, throwing his

bag onto his doorstep on the way. Mahala heard the thud of the bag hitting the doorstep and half-turned to see him approaching. They both called out, 'Hello,' at the same time, and began exchanging a few pleasantries, enquiring as to how each other was, and how their day had gone so far. This small talk over, Daniel came to the real reason for his wanting to speak to her.

'Erm, Mahala, I was wondering ... Would it be convenient for me to call on Charles and yourself sometime, maybe later this evening? I'd like to ask your advice about something which is foremost in my mind at the moment.'

Mahala, inquisitive as to what this important thing could be, and always glad of an excuse to offer hospitality, replied, 'Certainly, Daniel. You're more than welcome to come in right now if you wish. Charles is inside, and we are not terribly busy at the moment.'

Without hesitation, Daniel knew that no time like the present was probably the best option.

'Yes, please,' he answered, 'as long as you're sure it's not too much bother for you?'

'Most certainly not, you know we always have time for you,' she replied cheerfully. 'Come on in, we were just about to have a cup of tea, so please join us. We can have some biscuits I made earlier.' This made Daniel all the more pleased in having chosen this moment to speak to her.

They went inside, and it wasn't too long before Mahala appeared with the tea, along with several of her home-baked biscuits on a tray. She proceeded to hand them around, before sitting down beside Charles on a large drop-armed chesterfield, which they had recently bought. It was the first time Daniel had seen it, and he would have loved to have been able to sit on it, but with his skin and clothes full of dust and grime from the day's work, he knew this was no time to ask.

Daniel took a sip of tea and, desperately hoping he would remember everything he intended to say, he began to explain what was on his mind.

'For some time now I've been having ever growing feelings towards Mr Baker's daughter, Ruth. I'm thinking, or maybe I should say hoping she has similar feelings towards me. Therefore, I would like to make my feelings openly known to her. But there's one thing that's bothering me. Although her parents are always friendly towards me, I feel sure they'd have wanted better for their daughter than a ticket man like me. After all, if in the future we were to consider marriage ... Well, I fear it is unlikely that I'd ever be in a position to provide sufficiently for her. At least not in a way her parents would have envisaged for her. I've a good job at the work's kitchen now, and when the project is finished I'm sure I'll manage to find other such positions, but I know this is not really enough.'

Daniel cast his eyes to the floor for a moment, feeling a little despondent, then said, 'I need your advice, sir. Should I pursue my feelings for Ruth, or should I stop my feelings from taking me any further along this path, for fear of making a fool of myself and hurting Ruth in the process?'

Charles and Mahala glanced towards each other, with what seemed to be a knowing smile. This puzzled Daniel, but his puzzlement was soon answered as Charles replied, 'It's interesting you should mention this now. For it was only last week, when I was at Mr Baker's farm buying some eggs, that we were discussing the friendship between the two of you. For some time now, it's been clear to all of us that you've been enjoying each other's company.' Charles gave a teasing grin, then continued, 'You will be pleased to know, that during our conversation, Mr Baker indicated that he would not wish to stand in the way of such a friendship developing further between the two of you.'

Daniel's face lit up, and he exhaled with a sound of relief. Then, with a questioning tilt of his head, asked, 'Did Mr Baker say if Ruth had ever spoken to him, or her mother, about any feelings she may have had towards me?'

Charles smirked. 'No, I'm sorry, he didn't. I'm afraid you will have to find that out for yourself!'

Mahala uttered a short, interrupting, 'Ahem.' Then, gaining their attention, continued, 'Not this coming Saturday, but the following one, there is to be a concert and dance in Perth. Charles and I were intending to go, so maybe you would like to join with us. This would be a good opportunity for you to ask Ruth if she would like to come along too?'

'And I'd be delighted to buy the tickets for you both,' added Charles.

At hearing this, Daniel's excitement grew, and he could sense his trembling, causing the cup and saucer to chatter. He hastily put it down before spilling it, and said, 'Thank you for that very kind offer. I feel I don't deserve all the goodness you both keep bestowing upon me. Having said that, it's an offer I gratefully, and humbly, accept. Thank you.'

Not only were Daniel's hands now trembling, but his heart was fluttering too. This was a result of being handed such a good opportunity to see Ruth again and knowing that at some point, over the next day or two, he would need to pluck up the courage and actually ask Ruth if she would be willing to attend the dance with him.

Daniel got very little sleep that night. He lay awake for hours trying to come up with an appropriate form of words to say to her. He would need to say something enticing enough for her to accept his invitation without making her, or himself, feel uncomfortable.

Each time he came up with an idea he thought suitable enough, he would practise the sentence over and over again, wanting it to be word-perfect when the time came. But every time he thought he'd perfected it, doubts soon sneaked in, which resulted in him being unable to sleep through worrying about it. His main worry was that she'd be offended, would completely reject his advances, and never wish to speak to him again.

***

The following day seemed to take forever to go by. It was as though each minute of his working day was taking an hour, and each hour a day. In a bizarre sort of way, it reminded him of those dragging days when he'd been made to turn the crank back in prison. Of course this was only with the slowness of the day, not the with the pain and suppression of spirit the crank inflicted on him. For now he had that happy, loving feeling inside, mixed with a reoccurring butterfly tummy well known to lovers.

Daniel also knew that after his work was over, time would no longer be dragging. Indeed, it would probably be doing the opposite, racing ahead far too fast.

Eventually his working day ended, and he began making his way over to the store where Ruth worked.

Normally Daniel would be walking at a brisk pace, eager to reach the store as soon as he could. But on this occasion, despite his legs trying to do as they had always done, his mind was attempting to override things, causing him to dawdle. His legs wanted to get there, but his brain told him that the most sensible plan would be to hang on, so he could meet her outside after the store had closed. That way, he would be able to deliver his invitation without any interruptions or having nosy customers listening in. He also didn't want the owner of the store or the other man who occasionally worked there overhearing him.

The store owner came across as a pleasant man, and Ruth always spoke well of him. But Daniel was only too aware that making such a personal request at her place of work was not the thing to be done.

The other man who helped in the shop was Chinese. He had taken part in one of the Australian gold rushes several years previously. While panning, he had discovered quite a large number of nuggets. With his gains, he had moved to Perth, setting up a laundry business there. Unfortunately for him, the business had taken a downturn in recent times, so he'd taken a part-time job at the store.

Searching for gold had always been part of Daniel's plan, for when he eventually got his Certificate of Freedom. He had often entertained this idea as a way to get rich quick and find happiness. However, having spoken to Charles and others about it, he now realised it was probably more of a dream than a certainty that he would find enough gold to enable him to spend the rest of his life in happiness. If indeed finding gold would do that anyway. But still, he hadn't completely given up on the idea of finding that pot at the end of a rainbow.

Eventually Daniel arrived outside the store. Keeping slightly out of sight of the large bay window at the front, he sat down on the edge of the dusty street, waiting for Ruth to come out. Even though she wasn't due to leave for at least another half an hour, he still kept one eye towards the door in case she happened to leave earlier than expected.

Daniel had been sitting on the edge of the street for almost half an hour when he was unexpectedly startled by the sound of a harsh voice from behind him.

'What are you doing, sitting here on the street like this?'

Not having seen anyone approaching, Daniel's heart jumped into his mouth. He shot to his feet, seeing before him a tall, forbidding-looking man, in police uniform.

'You look like a vagabond or a convict,' remarked the policeman, sharply.

'No, sir, er, w-well, yes. But I've got my ticket-of-leave,' mumbled Daniel. He was shocked at how this policeman was able to tell his background by just looking at him. After all, it was not as if he was dressed in the prison's uniform.

The policeman scrutinised Daniel in disgust.

'Then you'd better show me your ticket, or I will be taking you back to the prison, right away. That's where your sort belong.'

Daniel reached into his trouser pocket for his ticket, which he had to carry with him at all times. It wasn't there. He reached into the other pocket, but it wasn't there either. He began panicking, coming over extremely hot and sweaty. He put both hands into his pockets at the same time, but nothing was to be found.

His whole world was now beginning to fall apart.

Not only would he be going back to gaol, there would now be no dance, and the chance of Ruth wanting anything to do with him again was going down the Swan River.

Just in time, he came to his senses. 'You idiot,' he mumbled to himself, and reached for the inside pocket of his coat ... the place where he always kept his ticket. Pulling it out, he smiled, handing it to the officer with a massive sigh of relief.

The officer inspected it closely, before handing it back without any change to his expression of disdain. 'I've been watching you for a while, lad. So why are you loitering on the streets – do you have any accommodation to go to?'

'Yes, I do, sir. I live with the Holt family ... Charles Holt. He works at the bank.'

Daniel was hoping the officer would have known him, as Charles held one of the more respected positions within the community.

The officer didn't show any sign of acknowledgement at this remark, and instead continued with his aggressive questioning.

'Why are you here, sitting on the street then, and not at home? I think you are up to no good. Maybe you've been drinking and should be taken back to gaol.'

'I'm not doing wrong, sir, nor have I been drinking. I'm waiting for someone,' replied Daniel, desperately hoping this reassurance would be enough to convince him.

The policeman looked behind and in front of him, in a rather theatrical manner, then said, 'Well, if that is the case, where are they then? What's this person's name?'

As Daniel went to reply, he heard the delightful, sweet sound of another voice close by.

'Hello, Daniel ... What is the matter, Constable?'

It was Ruth. Daniel was always pleased to see her, but never had he been more so than this.

'This is the lady I was waiting for,' stated Daniel firmly.

The policeman snorted. 'Is this true, Miss?'

'Yes, indeed it is, Constable. He was waiting here for me to finish work,' she replied, flicking her eyes towards Daniel, looking for confirmation that what she'd just said was correct. She was relieved to see him nodding his head in affirmation.

The policeman stared at Daniel, as if making a mental picture of his face, then slowly walked away from them, without further comment.

'What was that all about?' asked Ruth when the policeman was out of ears' reach.

Daniel shrugged his shoulders. 'He said that I was up to no good. Suggesting that I hadn't got anywhere to stay. I got the impression he has it in for ex-convicts.'

'You're right about that, Daniel, he has. But then, he doesn't like anyone ... especially those who were not born here. Anyway, try and forget about him. Mind you, it's probably best if you keep out of his way in the future

– he will definitely have it in for you from now on.'

Daniel huffed, 'Oh thanks, that's nice to know!'

Ruth raised her eyebrows with a smile. 'Anyway, it's nice to see you, but what are you doing here? Were you waiting for me?'

Daniel's heart gave a little skip, as he knew the time had now come to make his feelings known to her. He drew a deep breath, but completely forgetting all the things he had spent hours agonising over, he simply blurted out the first thing that came to his tongue.

'Yes, I was. Er, I was wondering if you would like to come to the dance with me?'

Ruth's eyes opened wide with surprise, as she certainly hadn't expected this invitation. Seeing her reaction, Daniel was sure he'd been far too forward, so he hastily added, 'Oh, I'm sorry, Ruth. I hope I haven't offended you?'

'No, I'm not offended. I'm very flattered ... and, yes, I would love to go with you ... Although there is one tiny little problem,' she replied, blushing a little.

'What is that?' Daniel asked cautiously, worried, wondering what answer was about to come.

Ruth gave a reassuring smile. 'The problem is ... I'm afraid I can't dance very well.'

Putting both hands to his forehead, Daniel slowly ran his fingers through his hair until they reached the back of his head. Ruth took this gesture as a sign of his frustration at her confession, but she needn't have worried.

'I've just realised something too,' replied Daniel. 'I can't dance very well either … Come to think of it, I've never been to a dance in my whole life.'

They both burst out into uncontrolled laugher. Partly through seeing the funny side of the situation, and partly to hide the self-consciousness which they were both now feeling.

After they had finished laughing, there was a short, slightly awkward silence, with neither of them knowing quite what to say next. Ruth was the first to speak.

'I'm afraid I must go home now. But I don't mind if you can't dance, so if you don't mind about me, then I'd be delighted to go with you.'

Daniel was over the moon with delight with her answer, and having said their goodbyes, they went off in opposite directions, both lost within their own thoughts of the forthcoming dance, and what might become of this ever growing relationship.

CHAPTER 27

The Dance

The evening of the dance came. As had been arranged, Charles and Mahala made their own way to the hall, while Daniel walked over to Ruth's home, and from there, her father kindly took them by horse and trap to the hall.

When they arrived, several folk were already there, either milling around outside or having already made their way inside the hall. Ruth and Daniel spotted Charles and Mahala sitting on a bench near the main door. They began waving enthusiastically, trying to catch their attention, which worked. Charles and Mahala immediately got up and began making their way over to them. As they were doing this, Daniel and Ruth both spotted a policeman standing near the doorway. This was not just any policeman, though, he was the one who had questioned Daniel outside the store. Not wanting to worry the other, neither Daniel or Ruth let on to each other they'd seen him, and they tried not to look at each other as they got down from the trap, in case their faces gave the game away.

'Thank you for bringing us here,' said Daniel,

reaching up to shake Mr Baker's hand.

'Have a good evening, both of you,' he replied. 'I will collect you at 10 o'clock. And remember, Daniel, best not to drink any alcohol. If anybody was to report you, it might be the end of your ticket.'

Although Daniel was perfectly aware of this, it was still a sobering remark, and yet again he was conscious of the fact that, although he was free, he was still not completely free to do as he wanted.

Charles and Mahala reached them, and after exchanging a few pleasantries with Mr Baker, said goodbye to him, and the four of them headed towards the hall. They had no option other than to walk past the policeman as they went, so Daniel kept his head down, trying to be inconspicuous. But as they passed, he was sure the constable's eyes were following him, and he was convinced that he'd been recognised. This left him feeling extremely uneasy, and for some time after entering the hall, he found himself constantly glancing back towards the door, fearing the policeman had followed them inside. But once they had taken their seats at one of the round wooden tables on the far side of the hall, he managed to forget all about the policeman and didn't let this beginning spoil the event.

The evening's entertainment started with a pleasant trio playing piano, violin, and cello. This was followed up by a song called 'Alice, Where Art Thou?' and a collection of songs that were sung by The Minstrels of the West. After this section of entertainment had concluded came the first dance, a waltz.

Thanks to a dance lesson from Mr Holt the day before, Daniel was able to lead Ruth onto the floor, having a little bit of an idea as to what he should do. Both he and Ruth made many mistakes during their dances, but this didn't deter them in the slightest. Indeed, it seemed to make the event all the more fun, and looking around them, they were far from alone with their missed steps.

The event was organised in two halves, with a break in the middle for some light refreshments. Both halves involved a mixture of songs and classical dances to partake in, and the evening finally came to an end with the playing of 'God Save the Queen'.

Daniel and Ruth had a wonderful evening together and were both most disappointed when the evening drew to a close and it was time to make their way back to their homes.

Outside, Ruth's father had arrived on time to collect her. Charles and Mahala began telling him all about the evening's entertainment, while Daniel and Ruth remained a few steps away, re-living some of the awkward moments they'd encountered during their dancing, and which they were still finding greatly amusing.

It didn't seem long before Ruth's father called over to them, asking Ruth to climb up on board. Ruth and Daniel said goodbye to each other, and as Daniel thanked Ruth for accompanying him, he stretched out his hand, hoping she would take it. She did, and Daniel gave it a gentle shake. Then, becoming ever more emboldened, he carefully moved her hand towards his face, stooping to meet it halfway, and gave the back of her hand a light kiss. As he moved his lips away, he checked to see her reaction. He was relieved to see her radiant smile glowing back at him. Ruth then leaned forward and whispered into his ear, 'Thank you for a lovely evening, Daniel. I've had such a delightful time tonight; I will remember it forever.'

She climbed up beside her father, and almost as soon as she'd settled herself down, they pulled off. Ruth turned around and continued waving at Daniel until they had disappeared out of sight.

Daniel, Charles, and Mahala walked home, talking most of the way about the lovely evening they had all enjoyed. During pauses in their conversation, Daniel could still hear those last words of gratitude that Ruth had whispered into his ear. Even after he had arrived back home, tucked up nicely in his bed, he could still hear them. It was almost as if she was there in the room.

Over the next few months, the relationship between the two of them grew ever stronger, and they began spending ever increasing amounts of time together.

CHAPTER 28

A Proposal

March 1870

It was a Sunday evening. Daniel had spent an enjoyable afternoon with Ruth and her parents at their home on the farm. Spending every other Sunday with them had now become almost routine, and he was feeling very much part of their family.

Having finished tea, they all retired to the sitting room, ready to commence their usual Sunday evening time of prayer and reading of the scriptures.

Daniel looked forward to this spiritual end to the evening, which would be led by Mr Baker. He would begin by reading from the Bible, then pose a question or two in connection with the passage of scripture they'd just read. Daniel always found these discussions most helpful in developing his ever increasing faith in God.

On this particular Sunday, it had been raining hard for most of the day, so after they'd concluded their time of religious reflection, Mr Baker suggested they all have a cup of cocoa, before taking Daniel home. Daniel was hoping for this offer, so he didn't refuse.

Having had their evening drink, Mr Baker got up, clearly on his way to fetch the pony and trap to take Daniel home in.

He was halfway across the room when Daniel called over to him, 'Er, before you go, sir, I have something I would like to say.'

Sensing Daniel had something important to say, Mr Baker sat back down.

'Carry on, lad, what is it?' he asked.

Daniel reached over, taking hold of Ruth's hand, which was resting on the arm of her chair. She gave him a hint of a smile, while raising her eyebrows up and down in support of what Daniel was about to say.

'I have something I wish to ask of you, sir,' he said rather nervously. 'I would like to ask for your blessing, that I may have Ruth's hand in marriage.' He paused again, hoping for a comment, but none came. He thought their faces were possibly showing a glint of pleasure, but he wasn't sure if this was just wishful thinking. He continued, 'Obviously I am still subject to my ticket restrictions, but I believe I'm right in saying this doesn't prevent my getting married. That being said, if you were to consent, but would prefer we wait until I have my Certificate of Freedom ... Then we are more than prepared to wait a further year, until my ticket-of-leave has expired. I have spoken to Charles about my desires, and he has suggested I should take your advice on this matter. Which I ... we are both more than happy to be guided by.'

Daniel gently bit his bottom lip and flicked his eyes towards Ruth for approval on how he'd done. She winked at him, flashing a smile, but at the same time, knowing it mattered not how she thought he'd done, it was what her parents thought that counted.

Mrs Baker had now developed a clear smile of approval. Mr Baker's face on the other hand was giving nothing away. He stood again, straightening his waistcoat as he rose. Daniel and Ruth feared the worst from the response that was about to come. There followed what seemed to be an age of silence in the room. Although in reality it was probably no more than four or five seconds.

All were now staring at Mr Baker, bracing themselves in readiness for his reaction. Slowly a smile began to appear. 'Nothing would give me greater pleasure than giving to you my daughter's hand in marriage. If this was to be within the year, then I'd prefer you wait until the very end of the year. I say this, as it would be far better if you found another form of employment first, with a better income, and were settled in that position—'

'My thoughts entirely, sir,' interrupted Daniel. Even though he knew that finding such a new job would be no small task, even an impossible one.

Mr Baker took his seat, relaxing into the chair, which in turn helped Daniel and Ruth feel a little more at ease.

'Actually,' continued Mr Baker, 'we have been

anticipating for a while that you would be asking for Ruth's hand ... My wife and I have talked at length about all the implications this would bring, and we have come to the conclusion that the best way forward would be for you to come and work here on my farm. This would enable me to increase my livestock numbers, and hopefully this would make the extra money needed to pay for your wages.'

Daniel and Ruth were stunned at what they were hearing, yet there was even more to follow. 'Further to this, I will also begin preparations for having a small marital home built for you both here on the farm.'

Daniel and Ruth looked at each other, dumbfounded, with their eyes and mouths wide open in happy disbelief. Daniel knew their reactions were clearly showing absolute delight and pleasure at this generosity, but Daniel knew that their reactions were not enough, and he needed to respond by verbally expressing his gratitude to them.

Daniel went over to Mr Baker and shook him by the hand. 'Sir, this is more than generous of you. I truly will never be able to thank you enough.' He took two deep breaths to compose himself, before tentatively adding, 'Back in England, Christmas is a rather popular time to get married. Would you see that as an acceptable length of time to wait?'

Mr Baker briefly considered Daniel's suggestion before saying, 'I think the first thing to do is to organise your change of employment. I'm sure this can be easily worked out, within a week or two, then you can start working on the farm. We can assess how things are going over the next few months. So, perhaps it would be wise for us to make a decision after that.'

'I fully agree with your wise words, sir. And I say again, thank you for everything. I promise I will work hard and do all I can to prove your goodness towards us was well placed,' answered Daniel reassuringly.

'Oh, I'm sure this will prove to be the right decision for us all, and the business too,' said Mr Baker. 'Oh, and one more thing … there is no need to keep addressing us so formally. Please, from now on, it's Joseph and Ellen.'

***

Daniel was true to his word and worked hard, and relatively easily grasped all of the things he was asked to do. During his childhood, Daniel's father had kept a few chickens in their garden. Daniel felt sure it was due to this that he was able carry out his work with such ease. This hadn't gone unnoticed by Joseph, who was extremely impressed with Daniel's keenness and, more importantly, the efficiency he showed.

CHAPTER 29

A Happy Wife, A Happy New Home

It was on Christmas Eve in 1870, the anniversary of his entry into Fremantle Gaol, that Daniel and Ruth became man and wife.

They began their married life living at Daniel's lodgings, as the house which Ruth's father was having built for them was still to be completed. The work had begun in early September, but they always knew it would never be ready for their wedding day. Even so, things progressed at a good pace, and they were absolutely delighted to move into their lovely new abode, on the far side of the farm, in early February. It was a lovely two-bedroomed lodge with a corrugated tin roof. It also had a delightful wooden veranda at the front, with three wooden steps leading up to the front door.

On their first evening in their new home, they sat on the veranda, quietly drinking a cup of tea while gazing out across the farmland, as the sun slowly disappeared beyond the horizon. In the distance they spotted three Noongar youngsters, probably young teenagers, who were stalking – or at least trying to stalk – a mob of kangaroos. Daniel loved the sight of kangaroos. Even though he had seen many of them since his arrival in Australia, he still found them amusing creatures to watch, and the scene unfolding before him seemed even more amusing.

The three Aboriginal lads, armed with their Dowak sticks, were still some way off when the kangaroos spotted them. Off they bounded, with the three lads in futile pursuit, getting further and further away with every bounce they made. They were soon out of sight, and their pursuers turned tail with heads bowed down, unsurprisingly returning home without their trophy.

After this spectacle was over, Daniel and Ruth settled back down, peacefully enjoying their relaxing evening. Daniel's memories began drifting back to his old life back in Great Hadham.

It would be winter there now, he thought to himself. *It would be dark, and either freezing cold or dreary and wet. And I would be hungry and tired after a hard day's work ... Assuming I had work.*

He took hold of Ruth's hand, gave a contented sigh, saying softly, 'I love this life, and I love you, Ruth.'

Ruth looked lovingly towards him. 'And so do I, Daniel, very much indeed.'

As she was saying this, she noticed Daniel's smile slowly fade. His eyes cast towards the ground, staring blankly, without blinking.

'What is the matter ... Are you alright?' she asked.

Daniel said nothing. Ruth assumed he'd not heard her, so she asked again, 'Daniel. What is the matter?'

He still remained quiet, so Ruth squeezed his hand. He came to, his smile spontaneously returning.

'Oh, I'm sorry, there's nothing the matter. Only I've just remembered something ... It was actually seven years ago, on this very day, that I set light to that stack.' Daniel blew out his cheeks and said, 'Those seven years have been very long and hard for me. But having this life here, especially with you, means it's all been worth it ... My life has turned out far better than I ever imagined.'

Daniel then gave a loud gasp. 'I've just remembered something else ... What with the wedding, my work, and moving here, I'd completely forgotten that—'

'Forgotten what?' interjected Ruth.

Daniel jumped out of his chair, laughing. 'Next month ... It's next month that I will finally get my Certificate of Freedom. I will no longer be a ticket man ... At long last, I really will be free.'

Ruth leapt up, flung her arms around Daniel's neck, and they both stood on the veranda, entwined, holding each other in a long, long embrace. Neither of them saying anything. There was no need, as the hug was saying it all.

CHAPTER 30

Freedom

At nine o'clock in the morning, on the twenty-second of March 1871, Daniel and Ruth were picked up by her parents in their horse and trap, and they headed off to the local magistrates in town. When they arrived, they were met outside by Charles and Mahala. Then, once the horse had been tethered securely, the party went inside. They didn't have to wait long for the formalities to be completed, and at long last Daniel finally received his Certificate of Freedom. After seven years of confinement, and restrictions on his movements, he really was now a free man.

Afterwards they all went back to Joseph and Ellen's home, for a family celebration. The table had already been laid out in the front room with an array of lovely food. Meats, sandwiches, slices of cake, and home-made biscuits adorned the table. Most of which had been covered with a variety of plates, bowls, and towels, to prevent any flies from starting the feast before they arrived back.

Ellen went into the kitchen to make pots of tea and coffee, while Ruth began taking the covers off the food, which was accompanied by a host of anticipating sounds and delighted remarks.

Ellen soon returned with the drinks, placing them on a side table, which already had several cups on it. Also on the table were six wine glasses, also waiting with anticipation of being filled.

Joseph handed everyone a glass, and the room fell silent as he took a bottle of wine out of a cabinet, removed the cork, and began filling each glass. The eyes of all in the room were on him as he then began to address the gathering.

'Before we start eating, I would like to propose a toast ... Ladies and gentlemen, please raise your glasses, to Daniel and to his new life of freedom.'

Everyone joined in the toast, apart from Daniel, who was staring into his glass of wine.

Ruth nudged him. 'Say something,' she prompted.

Daniel lifted his head, put the glass to his nose, and took a long, lingering smell of the wine, before beginning his reply of thanks.

'Other than during the storms at sea, I've not had a drink of alcohol for many years. Indeed, it was on the morning I fired the stack that I last enjoyed a drink. A mug of beer from Harrington's beerhouse ... Now, seven long years later, I am about to have my first proper drink.' Daniel stopped to compose himself before carrying on. 'I want to thank every one of you here, for all that you've done for me over the past few years. For giving me homes to live in, work, and putting your trust in me. For all these things, and much more … I will be forever grateful to you.'

He blinked hard, sensing that his eyes were in danger of becoming a little watery. 'You have all helped to give me such a wonderful new life here. It was the kind of life I'd often dreamed of having, while back home in England, but there have been many occasions since when I was convinced my dream would never be fulfilled. But here I am, truly living this dream, and it's thanks to everyone here in this room that I've made it … So, I would like to propose a toast of thanks, from me to all of you … Thank you, to all of you.'

Daniel raised his glass and began taking his first drink of alcohol as a free man in seven years.

Everyone joined in the toast and began a prolonged round of applause. When they'd finished, Ellen handed Daniel a plate, inviting him to be the first to commence the feasting. This he did with haste, followed just as eagerly by the other guests.

A pleasant time of chatting and eating was had by all, until shortly after one o'clock, when Daniel remembered he'd a farm to run, and the livestock wouldn't look after themselves. They brought the party to a close, and after thanking everybody yet again, Daniel left. He was the first to leave his own freedom party, which he found more than a little amusing as he went on his way.

***

Three hours later, his work completed, Daniel began strolling back towards his home. As he was crossing the farmland, he looked up to the sky, turning from left to right and behind him. It was an interesting mixture of sun and clear blue sky in one direction, increasing clouds from another, and further around there were dark, ominous rain clouds. Looking towards the front again, he could see his house, but now, arching over its roof was a large, brightly coloured rainbow.

The appearance of this stopped him in his tracks as he began recalling that special day in Chatham Prison when, at his very lowest point, he spotted a rainbow through the window. The sight that day had given him the essential uplift he needed, and with it, the determination to keep heading towards his dream.

Once again, Daniel was witnessing the significant sight of a rainbow. This time, he felt it was like a banner over his house. A banner that was celebrating with him the first day of his freedom.

The vision before him was now becoming too much to take in. He was sure the rainbow had been placed there by God, as a sign that although he'd done wrong in the past, God had clearly not deserted him throughout his time as a convict, and was still with him now. Tears began to roll down his face. Tears resulting from a multitude of mixed emotions. He dropped to his knees, thanking God aloud, completely unaware of his surroundings, or whether anyone could see him. Even if they could, he cared not.

Having finished his prayer of thankfulness, he remained kneeling, watching the rainbow as it began to fade. After it had disappeared, he got up and ran all the way home. Propelled by the excitement of what he had just witnessed and an unstoppable desire to share his experience with Ruth as soon as possible.

CHAPTER 31

A Face from the Past

Life continued to go well for Daniel. He was increasingly given more responsibilities and involvement in the running of the farm, and it continued to flourish. In fact, things had been going so well that not many years had passed before Joseph allowed Daniel to run most of the farm by himself. He also had a large barn and two smaller ones constructed near to Daniel's house. This meant he was able to increase the livestock further, and Daniel didn't have as far to walk each day to look after them.

A short time after these changes had been made, Joseph began to develop a few health issues with his breathing. As a result of this, he offered to sell the farm stock to Daniel for a generously small sum of money. Of course, Daniel lacked the finance, but with help from Charles Holt, he was able to borrow the money from the bank.

It was around this time that Ruth gave up working in the store. This enabled her to spend more time running the home, and help out on the farm when needed. Having been raised on the farm, she was well used to this kind of work, and had enjoyed it too. Fortunately, she still did.

Daniel and Ruth loved their life together on the farm. Everything was running smoothly, and without any major incident. At least, that was until one Sunday in April 1887.

Daniel and Ruth had been relaxing inside their home when a loud knock came from the front door. Daniel opened it to see a policeman standing there. He could tell by the sombre look on the policeman's face that something was wrong, so he invited him in. As Daniel was closing the door, a fear began to set in.

Daniel hadn't knowingly done anything wrong, but having spent so many years in gaol, where every movement would be scrutinised by the suspicious eyes of the law, having this officer at his door made him feel incredibly uneasy.

'What's the matter, Constable?' he asked hesitantly.

The constable took off his helmet. 'Two of our men went to arrest a man who'd stolen some tools and dynamite from a quarry. He managed to escape, but in doing so, he shot Constable O'Connell. Tragically, our man has now died.'

Ruth gave an audible gasp, putting her hand to her mouth.

The constable continued, 'The incident occurred to the north of Fremantle, but the murderer could have fled anywhere, and will undoubtedly be looking for outlying farm buildings to hide out in … So until he's apprehended, I suggest you keep all of your doors and windows securely locked at night. You must also be extra vigilant, keeping a close eye on all your outbuildings. So beware, and if you do see him, don't try and capture him. He's very dangerous. Come straight to the police station. This man could kill again.'

'What does he look like?' asked Daniel.

'He's a stout fellow, about twenty years old, and around five feet ten inches tall, name of Hughes,' replied the constable.

Daniel thanked him for the warning, and without further ado, the constable went on his way to warn other residents in the vicinity.

For several nights following, Daniel and Ruth barely managed any sleep for fear of this murderer who was now at large. Daytime was equally nerve-wracking, and Daniel was highly cautious while working around the farm, in case the fugitive had chosen one of his barns to hide out in.

The following Saturday, Ruth went into town for some shopping, as was often the case on a Saturday. When she returned, it was not only with groceries but with several dramatic rumours about the shooting, and the possible whereabouts of the murderer. Some of these stories gave Daniel and Ruth even more cause for concern that night, but thankfully most of these tales were dispelled a few days later, after reading reports in the local newspaper.

For the first month following the shooting they remained very tense and on edge, but as the weeks went by, they, like many others in the community, began to relax, assuming that by now the killer was probably far away.

A few of the local folk were somewhat disappointed by this notion though, as there was now a reward of two hundred pounds for helping in his capture, and the money, as well as the fame for finding him, seemed very appealing.

By June, there was little gossip to be heard on the escaped outlaw. Strangely, what talk there was wasn't all against him. In fact, in some folk's eyes, he had become a kind of folklore character, akin to Ned Kelly.

Early one morning, towards the end of June, Daniel awoke as usual at the crack of dawn, had a quick cup of tea, then made his way over to the new barns where the chicken feed was kept. As he entered, he noticed a foot poking out from behind a stack of feed bags. He could see by the angle of the foot that it belonged to somebody lying down, who was probably asleep. Instantly Daniel remembered the escaped killer, Hughes. His heart began pounding as he carefully, and as quietly as he could, began stepping backwards towards the door.

He had only taken a few steps when the person behind the sacks began stirring. From the corner of his eye, Daniel spotted a pitchfork leaning against a post, within arms' reach. He instinctively grabbed it and, in the same motion, ran towards the feed bags, and jumping on top of them, he lunged the pitchfork forwards, firmly placing its tines on the chest of the startled, scruffy bearded man who had been lying asleep on the ground.

The man grabbed the bottom of the handle and began to struggle, trying to wrestle it away from his body. Daniel, having the upper hand, pushed the tines more firmly into the man's chest and hollered, 'Keep still, or I'll kill ya.'

This threat was enough for the man to cease the struggle, and he stretched out the palms of his hands in an act of surrender.

Daniel slowly slid down from the stack of feed bags, while still keeping the pitchfork against the man's chest. On the ground, between himself and the man, Daniel spotted a small canvas bag. Fearing it may contain some form of weapon, he briefly let go of the pitchfork with one hand, grabbed hold of the bag, and tossed it a little further away, out of harm's reach.

'Who are you?' demanded Daniel, grasping hold of the pitchfork with both hands again.

The man, knowing the game was up, answered, 'I'm the wanted man ... Thomas Hughes. So go on then, kill me, and get your reward. But, please, make it quick.'

'I'll only kill you if you try to escape. So don't try it,' replied Daniel, in a matter-of-fact tone. Although in saying this, he wasn't sure if he could have actually carried out this threat. Unless his own life depended on it. Unfortunately, given the circumstances before him, he was already well aware that things could easily unravel and turn out this way.

Thomas began to chuckle, which seemed a most bizarre reaction for the situation they were in, leaving Daniel feeling completely bewildered.

'What's so funny?' Daniel snapped.

Thomas stopped laughing. 'I think I've seen you somewhere before. You're one of those British convicts, aren't you? So really, you are no different to me. After all, one sin is the same as another in God's eyes, and I bet you tried to escape capture, too. Eh?'

This comment hit home but, grinning back, Daniel said, 'Yeah, you're right, I was a convict, but you couldn't be more wrong about me trying to escape.' Daniel stopped grinning. 'Now sit up.'

Thomas shuffled around on the ground, trying to sit himself upright, while Daniel was still maintaining a tight grip on the pitchfork.

'So, why did you do it? Why kill that constable?' demanded Daniel.

'I didn't mean to kill him. I only intended to frighten him off,' replied Thomas, briefly shutting his eyes before adding, 'The constable I shot was an old schoolfellow of mine. His father was a Pensioner Guard, the same as my father had been. We both knew each other and I'd no intention whatsoever to kill him.'

Hearing this caused Daniel to stiffen, his eyes flicking side to side with each blink he made. There was something in the back of his mind attempting to come to the fore. He couldn't think what it was, possibly an event, maybe something that had happened to him in the past. Then with a flash it came to him ...

'Your father. Is he also called Thomas?'

'Yeah. He died a few years ago.'

Daniel didn't reply straight away, as he attempted to process this information. He probed a bit further, 'And your mother ... Is her name Caroline?'

Thomas replied with a frown, 'Yeah ... So did you know them?'

Daniel began to laugh, much to the bemusement of Thomas.

'What is so funny?' he asked.

Daniel took a small step back from Thomas and, removing the pitchfork marginally away from his chest, said, 'You were born on a convict ship, the *Corona*, weren't you?'

Thomas looked surprised. 'Yeah. At least that's what they tell me. So were you a convict on that ship, then?' enquired Thomas.

'More than that, young Thomas, I saw you even before your father did ... I was a trusted convict on board, helping the ship's surgeon. I saw you being born!' chortled Daniel.

As this information began to sink in, Thomas joined in the laughter.

'So it's true, then. I've heard this story before, from a friend. His father was also on the ship as a guard. I presumed it to be true, but when I asked my parents, they denied it.'

'Oh, it's true, I can promise you that,' grinned Daniel.

Thomas became serious again. 'Well, I can't jump and kill you now, can I? Guess it's your lucky day ... So what are you gonna do? Kill me with that pitchfork, or take me alive to the police station and get your reward? I've seen the posters. There's a nice big reward.'

As he said this, Daniel remembered that on the day when he'd set fire to the stack, he had suggested to his friend, Levi, that he could hand him in for a reward. Levi had turned this opportunity down without hesitation, but right now Daniel didn't know what to do. After all, this man hadn't simply set fire to a stack, he was a murderer.

Daniel's decision would have been made a lot easier if Thomas hadn't just made the point about how God looks upon sin. Adding to that pressure, an old Bible verse had sprung to mind. The one which said something like 'Let he who is without sin cast the first stone'.

All this was a massive challenge to Daniel as he began considering the reward offer. It all sounded very tempting. On the other hand, he was now more financially comfortable than he ever thought he would be, and although not rich, he was happy with his lot.

Daniel knew he needed to do something, as he couldn't remain in this situation all day, and Thomas was still a killer, not to be trusted. It was obvious that being outside in the open would not only be a lot safer, but hopefully someone would be able to spot them and come to his aid. So Daniel ordered Thomas to get up.

Thomas was around the same height as Daniel, but bigger built, and although Daniel had the pitchfork in hand, he knew it wasn't the sharpest of weapons he could have been armed with. He also realised that although having no desire whatsoever to kill him, he knew he couldn't afford to show any sign of weakness. One sign of this, and Thomas would undoubtedly attack him, and as he clearly had that fight or flight mentality, this could well cost Daniel his own life.

Daniel straightened up, spreading out his shoulders in an attempt to make himself appear a more opposing figure. Then, with a strong air of authority, he pointed towards the door with his pitchfork, saying, 'Right, you go in front of me. We're heading to the police station. I'll make my mind up on the way what I'm gonna do. I may even let you hand yourself in … Maybe that way you'll not hang.' He added the last comment hoping it would give Thomas a glimmer of hope, and therefore not attempt any escape, especially a violent one.

Thomas began walking slowly towards the barn door, with Daniel right behind him, pressing the pitchfork into his back with enough force to make him conscious it was still there.

Thomas stepped outside, and in doing so, he kicked his foot backwards, hard, onto the partly open barn door, causing it to slam onto the pitchfork, sending it spinning to the ground. With that, Thomas swung around, smacking Daniel full in the face with the palm of his hand, causing him to fall backwards into the barn.

For a brief moment Daniel was left stunned and disorientated, but regaining his senses, he scrambled to his feet double quick.

Thomas had already begun running away. Daniel shouted at him to stop, and to his great surprise, Thomas obeyed the order and turned around. Daniel thought, or at least hoped, he was about to raise his hands in surrender. Unfortunately this optimism was very much misplaced. Thomas reached for his inside pocket and, producing a gun, pointed it in Daniel's direction.

Without hesitation Daniel dived back into the barn and hit the floor, waiting for a shot to ring out. He held his breath ... No shot came.

Worried that Thomas may now be heading back to the barn, Daniel gingerly peered around the door. He was relieved to see that Thomas was not only fleeing in the opposite direction, but he was also heading away from his house and, most importantly, away from Ruth.

Daniel got up and dusted himself down. Although in great shock at the dramatic situation which had just unfolded, he still managed a grin, thinking, *Oh well, whether I wanted it or not, there goes my reward.*

Daniel kept his eyes on Thomas until he was far off into the distance before hastily making his way back home. When he got back to the house, he burst through the back door with such speed it made Ruth jump. She was washing up, with her back towards the door, and this sudden intrusion caused her to drop the plate she was washing back into the bowl. Thankfully without causing any damage.

Ruth could tell at once by Daniel's expression that something was wrong, but before she had chance to enquire, he'd already begun telling her all about his eventful start to the day. After he had finished telling the tale, they wasted no time in hitching up the horse and driving to the police station to report the morning's drama.

A few days later a policeman called. To their relief, he informed them that Thomas had now been captured, although he had been slightly wounded during yet another shoot-out.

CHAPTER 32

A Happy Birthday

Back in the winter of 1864, Daniel had been unable to think of anything positive about his current circumstances, or his future life. He couldn't wait to escape life in Great Hadham and head across the waves.

Now, with the passing of time, he would occasionally reminisce on some of the happier times he'd enjoyed back home, and he began to realise that not everything had been as bad as he'd once thought. He also wondered how his life may have turned out had he not taken the path he did. Once or twice he also wondered if it may not have turned out quite as bad as he once feared. Regardless of this, Daniel still had no doubts that overall his life would have been unbearable had he kept those matches in his pocket, and he still had no regrets whatsoever, having taken that path.

Although happy, Daniel and Ruth would have loved to have had the additional blessing of children, but this was never to happen. This was a disappointment to them, but they firmly believed it was all in God's hands, and they didn't let it stop them enjoying every moment of their life together.

Daniel's contentment with his lot was high, and those awful waves of depression, which had often reared their ugly heads, had now become a thing of the past. However, this contentment did take a dip during the spring of 1890, at the time of his fiftieth birthday.

On the morning of his birthday, Daniel awoke to find Ruth had already risen. Without needing to look at the clock, he could tell by the light coming through the shutters it was time to get ready for work. He lay there for a minute or two longer, thinking about his birthday, and listening to soft sounds of Ruth moving around in the other room. Even though it had been many years since he'd been locked away in Fremantle, he still enjoyed waking up, knowing that his thoughts weren't about to be drowned out by the ringing of a loud bell and warders shouting.

Daniel got up and went into the living room. Ruth had already laid out his breakfast on the table and was waiting for him with a big smile. She wished him a happy birthday, and as soon as he'd sat down, she produced a small box from her pinafore pocket. She placed it beside his plate and gave him a kiss on the side of his cheek. He gave a curious look towards the box before opening it, to reveal a nice, shiny new fob watch. He was absolutely thrilled with his gift, and his face shone with utter delight. He was especially pleased as his current watch, which wasn't new when he'd bought it, had become extremely scratched and battered over the years.

Ruth had also made Daniel a birthday card. This

was already on the table, propped up against his cup. He carefully picked it up, studying it, paying special attention to all the lovely words which she had written on the other side of the card.

Greeting cards had become increasingly popular things to send, especially Christmas cards. Although they had never received any themselves, some of their close friends had. One had been sent by someone who lived not five miles from where Daniel had been born. He recognised the name of the sender as being the owner of a large mansion from a country estate in that village. He didn't know them in person, but he knew a girl from Hadham who had gone into service there, just the summer before his arrest.

After Daniel had finished his breakfast, he went off to do his morning's work, returning as usual at around midday for his lunch. To his great surprise, he arrived home to find that Ruth had not only invited her parents but also several of their friends to join them for lunch, including the Reverend Alderson. Since leaving prison Daniel had met him on a few occasions, mainly when the Reverend had visited the Holts. But since Daniel's marriage, he'd seldom seen him, but it was always a pleasure to Daniel when he did.

Daniel was also pleased to see Charles had been invited too. Even though this was tinged with some sadness, as his lovely wife, Mahala, had sadly passed away the previous year.

Ruth's surprise birthday celebration for Daniel

made his day a very special one, and his delight was plain for all to see. However, over the next few days his mood began to change. His normal cheerfulness began to wane, and he became noticeably quieter and more withdrawn. Ruth began to feel somewhat concerned about him, especially as his normally light-hearted, happy-go-lucky nature had almost disappeared.

A week later Daniel and Ruth were relaxing on the veranda, watching the evening sun setting, and listening to the noise of a small flock of white corellas in nearby trees. After a while the birds settled down, and Ruth decided it was time to broach the subject of Daniel's low mood of late.

'Daniel, what has been bothering you these past few days?'

'Nothing,' replied Daniel, looking away, pretending to study something in the distance.

Ruth pursued the matter. 'There is something, Daniel, I know there is. You've not been yourself these past few days.'

Daniel remained quiet, now looking down at the ground, trying to think of what to say. Eventually he responded. 'I had a really lovely day on my birthday. It was perfect. Trouble is, now that I'm fifty, I seem to have been thinking more about my past life ... I can't help wondering what it would have been like if I'd remained in Hadham. I know I'd have spent most of it being miserable and working for someone else. I'd certainly never have owned my own farm. My health would have suffered with the British weather and lack of a decent meal. In fact, I may well have expired by now.' He finished speaking, lifting his gaze from the ground, back to the horizon.

'I don't understand, Daniel. Surely this should make you happy with having such a better life here?' stated Ruth with an inquisitive tone.

'Oh, it does. It makes me very happy.' Daniel smiled at Ruth tenderly. 'I'd never have found such a wonderful wife as you back there, that's for sure.'

Ruth gave a bashful smile. 'So what's the matter then?'

Daniel focused his eyes on the ground again, thinking for a moment before replying, 'I can't help but wonder what's happened to all my family over the years ... What their life is like now, or even if they are still alive? Because of her age, my mother may well have passed away by now. Then again, maybe not – she was a strong woman ... But that's the problem, I don't know anything at all about any of them.'

Ruth took Daniel's hand. 'Why don't you write to your mother? Even if she has now passed away, somebody who still lives there might write back, informing you of this. Or if not, they might be able to give the letter to someone who knew her. And it's quite likely that one of your brothers, or your sister, will still be living in the village.'

Daniel sat back in his chair, staring towards Ruth's hand which was still on top of his. 'I've already thought about doing this. But a letter would take such a long time to arrive. By the time I received a reply, if I ever got one, many months will have passed, and I don't want to wait that long.' He looked at Ruth, hoping for some sort of response, but guessing she couldn't think of anything reassuring to say, he added, 'And assuming my mother is still alive, and hasn't completely shunned me, I reckon the rest of my family will have done so by now. And as my mother is not that literate, she might not want to ask them to help her read it, and so she would probably just throw it away.'

'You are being rather defeatist, Daniel. This is not like you,' remarked Ruth.

Daniel put his other hand on top of Ruth's hand, and tentatively continued, 'Yes, maybe you are right … So in that case … how would you feel about us going to Britain? Only for a short time, of course. You've often said that you'd like to go there one day.'

'Oh, I would love us to go there one day. But we can't afford to do that at the moment, can we? And who would look after the farm when we're gone?' replied Ruth.

'We could hire some ticket men, and I'm sure your father will oversee the farm for us,' suggested Daniel.

Ruth twisted the ends of her shawl, thinking about what Daniel had just said. Daniel remained silent, giving her time to mull it over. After what seemed an age, she answered. 'No, I don't think we can afford that at the moment. But, please, write a letter to her. Or at the very least, think about it. Surely you have nothing to lose by doing so. It simply means you will need to be patient for a few months.'

Daniel slowly nodded his head in thoughtful yet unconvinced agreement, and they said nothing more on the subject for the rest of the evening.

The next morning, while they were having breakfast, Daniel brought up the subject again.

'I've been thinking, and you are right, Ruth, we can't afford to travel to Britain right now. So I have decided that I am going to do as you suggested and write a letter ... As you say, I have nothing to lose.'

'Well,' replied Ruth, 'I have been giving a lot of thought to this matter too. And although we can't both afford to visit Britain, why don't you go? ... On your own ... I'm sure we can borrow a little money from my father to help with the immediate cost.'

Daniel's eyes opened wide with excitement. A small grin tried to break through at the side of his mouth, but he held it back. 'Would you mind if I did that?' he asked, almost pleadingly, hoping she wouldn't retract her suggestion.

Ruth began to butter a slice of bread, as Daniel watched, waiting for her reply.

'No, I don't think I mind, but ...' She paused, trying to think how to tell him what was on her mind; however, Daniel couldn't wait.

'But what?' he asked anxiously.

Ruth finished buttering her bread before

continuing, 'I'm just worried that if you went back home … you would never return.'

'Don't be silly, Ruth. This is my home, here with you,' stated Daniel.

'Is it?' whispered Ruth, questioningly.

Daniel was about to reiterate what he'd said, but as he opened his mouth he was hit with a tidal wave of differing thoughts and emotions. So many, he didn't know what to say. The thought of going back to the old village where he grew up filled him with great excitement. As did the possibility of seeing his mother and the rest of his family again. He was in no doubt that he would return to Australia. He loved the farm and knew beyond any doubt that he would miss Ruth more than anything in the world. Yet, part of Ruth's question to him was still a big challenge. Was this new life, which he had gained through a great deal of suffering and pain over the years, really his home? More doubts flooded in. What if he travelled back and discovered that life in England had changed for the better? What if he arrived to discover that his mother, family, and friends were all still alive and welcomed him home like the prodigal son? Would he then find it hard to leave them, knowing that it would be most unlikely he would ever get another chance to see them ever again?

Daniel looked at Ruth. Seeing her sitting beside him, with that tender look in her eyes, was all he needed to see. He was convinced that his love for her was so deep that nothing could ever stop him returning. But as he was feeling reassured by this, another thought came to mind. What if something terrible was to happen to him on the journey? What if he became mortally sick or was lost at sea? So many thoughts were now bombarding his mind. It felt as if he was being tossed to and fro, like a convict ship in a storm.

Daniel placed his elbows on the table, covering his face with his hands, deep in thought, without saying a word or touching any of his breakfast.

Eventually he removed his hands from his face and opened his eyes. He hadn't noticed, but Ruth had already left the table and begun washing up her breakfast things. Daniel began picking at his own breakfast, but still eating very little of it. He then got ready for work, and after giving Ruth a gentle hug around her waist, saying how much he loved her, went off to work.

Daniel spent most of the morning deeply lost in his own thoughts. Deliberating and unable to concentrate properly on anything he did. Around midday he returned home for lunch, and as he opened the door to the kitchen, he saw Ruth standing in front of the oven, warming a pan of soup. She turned her head towards him, as he made his way over to her without saying a word. Reaching her, he put his head on her shoulder, and whispered into her ear, 'Thank you for being prepared to let me go and visit my homeland once again ... I've been pondering over it all day, and have finally decided that I won't be going back. I will do as you suggested and write a letter. I'll do it tonight, after dinner.'

Ruth stopped stirring the soup and put her arms around Daniel in a tight embrace, until disturbed by loud bubbling noises from the soup behind her.

That night, and after several failed attempts, Daniel eventually managed to complete a long letter to his mother. Then, after getting Ruth's approval as to what he had written, he tucked it behind a candlestick on the mantelpiece.

The following morning Ruth took the letter into town and posted it to 'Mrs S. Parker, or her family, Hadham Cross, Great Hadham in Hertfordshire. England'.

CHAPTER 33

Christmas at Home

Daniel had no misapprehensions. He knew it would take many months of waiting before he was likely to receive a reply to his letter. Assuming one was to be sent in the first place. He figured the earliest he was likely to receive a reply would be sometime in August, so he tried to put all thoughts on the matter to the back of his mind until then. Eventually August arrived, and the first thing he would do on arriving home from work would be to ask Ruth if any letters had arrived for him. Deep down he knew this was most unlikely, for if a letter had arrived, he knew Ruth would never have been able to contain herself and would have come looking for him post-haste.

August passed by without the arrival of a letter, as did September, October, November, and December. By the time the new year had arrived, Daniel had given up all hope of ever receiving a reply. Strangely, part of him was rather hoping that his mother had never received his letter. That way protecting him from the hurtful feelings of having been rejected by his mother and family.

Occasionally Daniel would entertain the idea of writing another letter, but each time he dismissed the idea. For exactly the same reasons he'd been reluctant to write a letter in the first place. He also considered the idea of putting sums of money aside each month, with the intention of saving enough to enable both himself and Ruth to make a visit to his homeland one day. He was very much tempted by this, but the overriding thought that his family were still angry with him and wanted nothing more to do with him was enough to stop him from doing this.

***

A year or two later, on Christmas Day, Daniel and Ruth went to the church in the morning, then afterwards, as had become the tradition, they went back to her parents' house for a nice turkey dinner. A turkey which they had reared themselves, on their farm. Around two o'clock in the afternoon they returned home, as the livestock still needed attending to, Christmas or no Christmas.

Daniel had been in good spirits all day, and they both laughed and joked all the way home. As soon as they arrived back, Daniel changed into his work clothes before going off to feed the chickens. Ruth stayed at home, making herself a drink and relaxing with a book. One which Daniel had bought her for Christmas.

She had expected Daniel to return after about an hour, but an hour and a half passed by without any sign of him. A little concerned, she put her book down and glanced out of the window behind where she was sitting. She spotted Daniel standing by a tree, about a hundred yards from their house. This tree stood on its own, and it was a place where Daniel would occasionally go if he wanted to be alone to think over any worries, or simply for a bit of peace and quiet. Because of this, Ruth thought little of it, returning to her book.

Another half hour passed by, and Daniel still hadn't returned. She took another look out of the window. He was still there, but now sitting under the tree with his back against its trunk. Although it was late in the afternoon, it was still warm and sunny, and he was sensibly sitting in the shade of the branches.

Ruth began to wonder why he hadn't returned. He'd never been there for such a long time before, and she couldn't think of anything particular that may have been bothering him. Although, over the previous few nights he had seemed a little restless. She had questioned him about this at the time, but he said it was nothing, he'd just been too hot to sleep. An answer she was not completely convinced of at the time, and was even less sure of now.

Ruth went to the kitchen, made two cups of coffee, and with both in hand, wandered over to join Daniel under the tree. He smiled as he saw her approaching. Ruth was relieved at this, seeing it as a sign that he wasn't overwhelmed with some major issue that she had been unaware of. She was still a little perplexed, though, as to why he was still there. Ruth handed him a drink and sat down cross-legged in front of him.

'What is the matter, Daniel? You have been here for ages.'

'Nothing's the matter, I'm fine. Just been thinking about things, that's all,' he replied, and after taking a couple of sips of his coffee, continued, 'I've been doing some more thinking about my family, Great Hadham, and all that stuff.'

'Oh no, not again,' said Ruth, frustrated. 'Look, why don't you just go back home to England? For two or three months maybe. I think this is the only way you will ever resolve this issue.'

Daniel shook his head. 'No, no, not at all. You don't understand … You see, I really don't want to go back there. I now know, deep down inside, beyond any doubt, that this here is my home … It really is. I have everything I've ever wanted here. My old village will always have a special place in my heart, and of course my family there, too. However, I can't really explain it, but I now have a strange feeling inside. A feeling of peace and contentment, regarding my old life, my family in Hadham, and my new life here … I know the grass would not be greener if I was to go back there … Well, I guess it will be greener because of the rain, but you know what I mean!' he said, tittering out loud at his own joke.

Ruth beamed with relief at hearing all this, and even though she thought her next question might push things too far, she still posed it.

'So, what about never seeing your family ever again?'

Daniel had just been asking himself the same question, so he knew the answer. 'I would love to know what has happened to them, and I now hope Mother received my letter. I want her to know how well my life has turned out ... The thing is, it's over twenty-five years since I last saw them, so I'm not sure that my family and friends from the village ever think about me now. Or will do so in the future. So I've come to the conclusion that it's pointless losing any more sleep over this matter, and furthermore, I no longer intend too.'

Daniel stood up, looking lovingly towards Ruth, and with his special smile said, 'If I was to go back, even if it was only for a few weeks, I would miss this farm and this country far too much. And most of all, I would miss you. Every single hour that I was gone, I would miss you, and all I have here ... Ruth, this is my home – everything I've ever wanted is here. This is my dream fulfilled. It's my pot of gold.'

Ruth jumped up, throwing her arms around Daniel's neck, and gave him a long, loving kiss.

After finishing their coffee, they slowly made their way back to the house, arm in arm. They had both enjoyed a lovely Christmas Day, made even more special by the way in which Daniel had just poured out the feelings of his heart.

Halfway back to the house, Daniel suddenly

stopped abruptly, jerking Ruth backwards. She glared at him with a surprised and partially cross look, wondering why he'd stopped so sharply. She didn't have time to ask, as he had already begun providing the answer.

'Ruth, I have also been wondering about something else.'

'What's that?' asked Ruth, not really sure if she wanted to know what answer was coming next.

Seeing her concern, Daniel promptly added, 'Oh, it's alright, don't worry – it's nothing bad,' then, giving his famous sideways grin to reassure her, continued, 'This Yuletide has been so wonderful. You decorated our house so nicely with the tree ferns and bits of eucalyptus. We've just had lots of wonderful food with your parents, and a nice glass of wine with it too! Furthermore, I've had some really lovely gifts. I love the jumper and cap your parents gave me. And I especially love the fountain pen with the gold nib that you gave me. It was such a generous gift—'

'I'm glad you liked it. And I love the gifts you gave me too,' Ruth said, butting in.

Daniel continued, 'I've been thinking about the last Christmas which I had with my family. That was a good Christmas. We had the top of a pine tree which had come from the farm where my brother worked. We decorated it with things my mother had made, and some others which my stepfather had bought. Then on that Christmas morning, after we'd been to church, we went back home for dinner. My sister had been given half a day off from the big house where she was in service, so she was able to join us, and we all had a lovely dinner together. Of course, it wasn't a big dinner like we ate today, but we did have things which weren't usually served up by Mother. We had a brace of pheasant, given to us by a farmer friend of our family. My mother had saved up enough money to make a plum pudding, then in the evening we had some sweets and nuts. Oh, and each of us had gifts. I remember getting a scarf which my mother had made, and my sister had embroidered my initial on a handkerchief. Later that day, the small boy who lived nearby came to show us what his parents had given him. It was a wooden Noah's ark with wooden animals inside. I remember it had two kangaroos. At the time I wondered if I'd ever get to see real ones, though I never truly thought I would,' he said with a smile. 'Of course it wasn't a new ark. His parents could never have afforded something like that, but he was still very excited with it ... Then in the evening, my father got out the magic lantern. One show was of a whale getting his revenge on a whaling ship. And another was a Christmas one, about Ebenezer Scrooge ... I remember lying in bed that night and thinking to myself, Christmas could never get any better than that day had been. I was wrong though. This one has been far better. Better than I could have ever imagined a Christmas could be.'

'Yes, it's been a lovely day,' nodded Ruth in agreement.

They carried on towards the house, and Daniel

began thinking out loud. 'I wonder what Christmas will be like in, say, fifty years' time. Or even in a hundred and fifty years' time.' He laughed. 'Maybe then, everyone will get more than a day off work, or the half day my sister got ... Maybe people will get two whole days off work, or even a week. Maybe children will get four or five toys, and not just one or two, and they would all be newly made ... Maybe everyone will have lots of gifts, and lots of food and drink – more than a person could possibly eat or drink in a day. Maybe everyone will have those Bonbon crackers that we had at your parents' today. Maybe—'

Ruth started laughing and interrupted him. 'Maybe lots and lots of toys, maybe lots and lots of food, maybe a week off work ... Daniel, I think you are taking your daydreaming too far again! This dream is one that will never come true.'

Laughing with her, Daniel agreed. 'Yes, I know. I am not really being serious. I know all that's impossible and will never happen.'

As he said that, he stopped laughing, narrowing his eyes as he briefly reflected on what he'd been saying, then said, 'You know, having said all these things are impossible, maybe ... just maybe, all this could actually happen one day.'

Ruth stopped laughing too, as she began to seriously consider the possibility of what he'd just said becoming a reality.

They reached the front door, and as Daniel went to

open it, Ruth said, 'If all of that was to happen, then I wonder if people would become so busy with everything going on that they would stop remembering why we have Christmas Day?'

Daniel laughed. 'Don't be silly, how could people ever forget the reason for Christmas Day!'

CHAPTER 34

Happy Christmas, Daniel

The family were sitting around the Christmas table. In the middle was a large plate, which had once held a Christmas pudding and a dozen mince pies. It was surrounded by several small jugs. These were now empty, but had contained fresh cream, soya cream, custard, and brandy butter. The remains of several Christmas crackers were strewn over the table, and on the floor stood two empty bottles of wine, one English and the other, Australian.

Stephen was sitting at the table, reclining as far back as he could without slipping off his chair. He had loosened his belt, and the top button of his trousers was undone, giving his tummy room to expand. Grandad George was sitting upright, with his chin on his chest, dozing in and out of sleep. A paper crown he was wearing had now slipped down, completely covering one eye.

Lesley and her mother-in-law were chatting about nothing in particular. Lesley, almost down to the bottom of her third glass of wine, had become noticeably more giggly and was pretending to ignore Stephen's looks of disapproval towards her.

The two children were in the lounge. Archie was playing with a remote-controlled car, a gift from his grandparents, and Abigail was half-watching the television while trying to put on various colours of nail glitter, a gift also given by her grandparents. She soon realised that her attempts to make her nails look as nice as her mum's, hadn't worked, so she gave up and flopped onto the settee to watch the film. This too was unsuccessful, due to all the sounds and motions coming from Archie and his remote-controlled car. Giving up with the television, Abigail started watching Archie's car going back and forth around the room, zooming under the chairs and crashing into walls. At one point she asked Archie if she could have a go. To her uttermost amazement, he allowed her to have a 'quick' go. It was a quicker go than she'd hoped, though, as the car had only gone a couple of metres when it got stuck between the leg of the coffee table and a pair of her grandad's shoes.

As it came to a halt, Abigail noticed the old letter, sent by Daniel all those years ago, was still on the table. She gave the remote back to Archie and carefully picked up the letter, attempting to make out some of the words, but without a great deal of success. This didn't seem to matter though, as she now knew the story about the person who had written the letter over a hundred years ago.

But it wasn't just knowing facts about Daniel that was special, or that he was an ancestor of hers. It was holding the letter in her hands, that gave her the feeling of having a real connection to the past, and especially to Daniel. It was as if she actually knew him.

Abigail looked over to her brother. 'I'm glad Daniel's mother kept this letter. It meant she must have still loved him.'

Archie was busy playing with his car again, and either hadn't heard her, or couldn't be bothered to answer.

Abigail focused on the letter again, staring at Daniel's signature at the bottom. She lightly stroked his name with her forefinger.

'Happy Christmas, Daniel ... You will never be forgotten.'

The end

HISTORICAL NOTES

(1)   Although now known as Much Hadham, the village had been previously known as Great Hadham.

(2)   The blacksmiths, mentioned on page 31, is now the village museum. *www.hadhammuseum.org.uk*

(3)   Records held at Fremantle Convict Establishment Museum, show that Daniel Phillips stood 5' 7 ½ '' tall, had dark brown hair, hazel eyes, and scars on his upper lip and thumb tip.

(4)   While on the run, Thomas Hughes became somewhat of a folklore figure, even gaining some sympathy with locals. He was convicted, not with murder, but manslaughter, and imprisoned in Fremantle. Six weeks later he attacked a warder, and escaped. However, this time he was quickly caught, and sentenced to receive thirty-six lashes from the Cat-o'-Nine tails, and to be kept in iron shackles for three years.

(5)   Thomas received his Ticket-of-leave in 1896, and in 1902 married Alice McLevie. He Died at the Claremont Hospital for the insane, in 1944.

(6)   The early morning bell at Fremantle Convict Establishment rang at different times during the year, according to season. Records from 1862 show that the bell rang at 5am from November 1st to February 14th, from February 15th until April 15th it rang at 5.45am, and for the rest of the year at 6am.

(7)   In 1846, William Crawford was appointed Assistant Surgeon on board the Royal Naval vessel, the Alligator, which

was hulked at Hong Kong. In 1861, he was appointed Surgeon Superintendent on his first convict transport ship, the Lincelles. He then served on four more convict ships, until his last crossing on board the Corona. William died in 1876, at the age of fifty.

(8)   Captain William Storey Croudace was born in Leeds, in 1821, and had his first command at the age of 21, sailing from Dundee to the Baltic. William's first voyage to Australia was to Melbourne in 1855, and afterwards he made several other journeys to Australia, before his record breaking trip on the Corona. In 1850, William married Elsie Stephen, daughter of the Scottish shipbuilder Alexander Stephen – owner of the Corona.

(9)   Richard Alderson (1821-1895) was ordained in 1846, and was chaplain of the Fremantle Convict Establishment for over twenty years.

(10) The Corona was a 1199 ton ship, built in Clyde, and classified as a 'clipper' ship with three masts, one deck plus poop, and a round stern. Her frame was built of oak and iron and was 209ft long and 35ft breadth. This journey to Australia was her maiden voyage; from there she went to Calcutta where she picked up over 400 Indian workers destined for the sugar-cane fields in Jamaica.

(11) In 1857, the Penal Servitude act abolished transportation, however it still continued until 1868.

THE AUTHOR

This is R.I. Maddams first work of Historical Fiction. He has previously compiled two Non-Fiction books. His first, 'Hadham's Headlines during the 1800s', was a collection of local newspaper articles, reporting events which took place in his home village of Much Hadham during the 1800's. His second book, 'Lest We Forget', commemorated the men from the village who lost their lives during the First World War.

While researching for Hadham's Headlines, he came across a newspaper report from 1864, telling of the arrest and trial of a young man from the village, who's plight 'Surviving the Waves – A Convicts Journey' is centred around.

R.I. Maddams was born in Much Hadham, and founder member of the Much Hadham History Society. Having lived most of his life in the village, he moved to Suffolk in 2017, where he began writing this book.

Before publication, 'Surviving the Waves' was entered into the New Anglia Manuscript Prize competition.

Discussion questions for your book club are available on his website: ***www.rimaddams.com***

Printed in Great Britain
by Amazon